"Unhand me this instant!"

Her voice, akin to a bucket of ice water down his spine, washed over him. He dropped his hands to his sides. "I only prevented you from taking a tumble, Miss Bryerly."

"You have no right to touch me. Get away from me!"

"If you think I tripped you on purpose to have an excuse to touch you, you're sadly mistaken."

"You have tripped me too many times as it is, and I beg of you to stay out of my way for the remainder of your life, and longer if possible."

He smiled at her murderous expression. "Really? You believe we might run into each other in the hereafter, in heaven?"

"Hardly that. I doubt that *you* will be going to heaven . . ."

Titles by Maria Greene from
The Berkley Publishing Group

THE BLACKHURST RUBIES
DARING GAMBLE
GENTLEMAN BUTLER
AN INCONVENIENT MARRIAGE
LADY IN DISGRACE
LOVER'S KNOT

The Fox Hunt
Maria Greene

JOVE BOOKS, NEW YORK

THE FOX HUNT

A Jove Book / published by arrangement with
the author

PRINTING HISTORY
Jove edition / April 1995

ISBN: 0-515-11590-8

A JOVE BOOK®
Jove Books are published by The Berkley Publishing Group,
200 Madison Avenue, New York, New York 10016.
JOVE and the "J" design are trademarks
belonging to Jove Publications, Inc.

PRINTED IN THE UNITED STATES OF AMERICA

10 9 8 7 6 5 4 3 2 1

One

SURPRISED, MISS JUSTINE Bryerly stared at the innocuous brown leather valise on the floor of the clothespress. She turned the fine piece of luggage, thinking it had to be a gentleman's article. Someone was now traveling sans his luggage and would surely curse long and loud when he discovered the valise had been left behind at the inn outside Crawley.

I wonder what could be inside, she said to herself as she fingered the handle. Her latent curiosity sprang to life. It would be impolite to snoop, but who was to know? *He must have left in haste, and if I but know what is inside . . . I might be able to help,* she rationalized even as she opened the valise.

A stack of shirts, some starched neckcloths, folded stockings—not much to get excited about. Underneath the clothing, she found a brown parcel tied with a string. Shutting off the inner voice cautioning her, she unwrapped the bundle.

She gasped as she came eye to eye with a thick roll of bank notes. There had to be at least a thousand pounds. Thoroughly shocked, she dropped the bundle on the bed and studied the brown paper. It was covered with strangely written symbols, and she could not decipher a single one.

Decipher. What if the valise belonged to a criminal? What if he found her going through his personal belongings? He might knock her down or even kill her for snooping into his secrets. She could almost hear her mother say: You're sticking your nose where it doesn't belong again, Justine.

Filled with sudden thoughts of self-preservation, she tied the paper around the bundle and stowed it into the valise and piled the shirts on top. Should she take this to the local authorities? As she debated with herself, she worried that she would end up involved in something sordid. Her parents would whisk her back home to Bath faster than a cat could blink, and that could not be borne.

She could give it to the landlord and explain that contents *might* be important. *He would be the most logical person to deal with missing valises,* she told herself. With a furtive glance over her shoulder, she set it on the floor.

Her maid, the prim and precise Agnes Trask, entered with a cup of tea. "Thought I heard you move about, miss. Strong tea will chase the morning cobwebs from your mind."

"Thank you, Agnes." Justine thought about the valise as Agnes helped her into a traveling costume of blue serge with a ruffled white collar and dark blue band edging the front.

The tea certainly made her eyes blink with less resistance and cleared her thoughts. Shortly, she would take the piece of mysterious luggage downstairs and forget about it. After making that decision, she resolutely shut away the speculations about the money and the strange symbols.

She sipped her tea and sat down so that Agnes could arrange her hair. She wished she did not have such trouble rising in the mornings. Late at night was when she sparkled the most. A shining, glittering diamond of the first water, her admirers called her, but she felt far from it. Her spirits had been low since Lord Lewington left London without as much as a good-bye, let alone an explanation for his behavior. She sighed and set down the cup. Not the slightest shard of sparkle remained in her heart.

Her hair brushed and coiled, and stuffed under a blue

bonnet with a feather-adorned poke front, Justine carried the valise downstairs. No ruffian was waiting to snatch it from her hand. Assaulted by the din of the guests waiting for the stagecoach, she handed it to the innkeeper.

"Mr. Winnow, I found this in my room, and it certainly does not belong to me," she almost shouted to make herself heard. "I glanced inside, and besides a stack of shirts and neckcloths, there is a peculiar brown paper parcel tied with a string." She paused to see if he would investigate, but he didn't. "Some unfortunate gentleman might miss his change of shirt this morning."

Mr. Winnow held up his hands in a gesture of surprise. "Dear me, it must belong to the young gentleman wot stayed 'ere the night afore last. E'll might be back for it."

"The article was inside the clothespress. You'd better send it on to his address." *If you have one,* she added silently. The valise had not been marked with the owner's name.

"You're right, Miss Bryerly," mine host said, scratching the bridge of his lumpy nose. He took the valise from her hand and smiled. "Thankee for takin' the trouble to bring it down, miss. I'll deal with it." He set it down beside a great heap of luggage. Right away guests started clamoring for his attention.

Justine had done her part. Curiosity still gnawed at her mind, but she returned to her room abovestairs to supervise her maid's packing of the few articles she'd used to freshen up before going to bed the night before.

She yawned behind her hand. She disliked rising at eight in the morning, but no one could sleep with the racket of stagecoaches and shouting ostlers in the inn yard. Not to mention loud patrons.

She looked out the window, seeing the northbound stage leave the inn. London bound, she thought, realizing that *she* had fled the capital and had no desire to see it for a long, long time. The city and its social whirl of balls and routs reminded her too much of the man who had claimed her heart during the season, which was now drawing to a close as the days grew hotter and the streets dustier. The foul smells coming from the river and the poorer parts of London had urged the upper ten thousand to retreat to the fresh country air of their estates.

Justine had two choices: to go home to her parents in Bath or to spend the summer with her sister, Honoria, who was enceinte and bored to flinders as she had no one to talk to except the servants. Lady Allenson's husband, Henry, was away on government business.

Justine had chosen to visit her sister. Nora was a prattle-box, rather trying at times, but entertaining and kind. Justine had agreed to go to Sussex rather than to face the questions of her mother. Mother had much too sharp eyes, and prying ways. *She would notice my dark-ringed eyes and drooping spirits,* Justine thought.

Justine disliked feeling sorry for herself; she disdained low spirits, but somehow she could not conjure up her usual good humor and enjoyment of life. She had always found a way to keep her spirits high, even when she had to jilt the Earl of Wyndham for lack of love. He had married her old friend Allegra Temple and now seemed very happy. Wyndham had been quite a catch, but Justine had long ago promised herself she would only marry for love, not position and wealth. Her friends pitied her for her ideals, but she had been right. Love had come—flashing like a bright comet, then dying abruptly.

Love had come tempestuously, in the form of Damien Trowbridge, the Marquess of Lewington. A rake who loved no one but himself, the dowagers had warned her, but had she listened? No, she had plunged into his riveting blue eyes and lost herself completely in his lazy wicked smile—until he one day told her he could not love. She had been so sure that he loved her, but he had denied any feeling deeper than affection.

He had told her about his lack of devotion, taking all the blame upon himself, but his rejection had still hurt as nothing had ever hurt before. He hadn't promised her anything; he hadn't approached her father, but a strong feeling had glittered in his eyes every time he looked at her. She had not been wrong on that score.

But *what* had glittered, was another puzzle altogether. She had been sure it was love, but now she realized she had misread him in the worst possible way. Surely, she knew what love was? Or had she been wrong all along?

"Oh, dash it all!" she cried out as the weight of her loss forced tears to her eyes.

"Miss Justine!" Agnes exclaimed, evidently shocked by such lurid language by her charge.

"I was only thinking aloud," Justine said, drying her eyes on the back of her hand in an unladylike fashion. But she did not have a handkerchief close by. Heaven knows, she had used them all to mop up her tears in the weeks since that dratted Lewington had left London.

He was the major reason she had reservations about visiting Nora in Sussex. His country seat, Ardmore Crest, was located no more than three miles from Milverly, Lord Allenson's estate. Sooner or later she was bound to encounter him, and he would believe she had followed him south to pursue their hopeless courtship.

"I don't blame him. In his shoes, I would think the same thing," she said out loud as she watched Agnes placing silver-backed brushes and combs into a traveling case of red leather.

Agnes gave her one of those long sideways glances she was prone to present at times like these. It was not the first morning that Justine had paced and muttered to herself as despair overcame her.

"If I may say so, miss, your sister will be pleased to have you at hand at Milverly. Her time is near."

"Four weeks, is it? Nora will need me since Mother cannot travel after her illness, but mayhap I ought to go home to Bath and forget that I was ever part of the London season."

Agnes shook her gray head. "Miss Justine, it's no use dwelling on the past. You must take interest in the future and put your distress behind you."

"You're right, but my mind seems to have a life of its own." Justine moaned, wishing she could sweep away her misery with a wave of her hand. "It haunts me, gives me sleepless nights."

Agnes hung her head, showing she was no stranger to grief. "We all have times of difficulties, Miss Justine."

Justine helped fold the towels she'd used last night. "I think it's time to leave this noisy hostelry and get on with our journey."

Instead of driving down to the coast in one day, they had left London late on the previous afternoon and stayed at the inn. Justine needed the time to adjust from the social whirl to the more quiet times ahead. Besides, she was in no hurry to arrive on Nora's doorstep, her ear to be the receptacle of her sister's incessant twitter. And she would have to endure probing questions.

Her time of gathering her senses was short enough, and once she reached Milverly, she would have to hide her true feelings. Nothing must upset Nora during her trying time.

Justine feared she would have to face Lord Lewington again sooner or later. Would he treat her with scorn or would he completely ignore her? Whatever the outcome, it would not be pleasant.

She shuddered at the thought and retied the bonnet strings under her chin too tight. Oh, for a heart with wings that could carry her away from misery. . . .

Pandemonium broke loose outside.

Damien Edward Lucius Trowbridge, the fourth Marquess of Lewington, of Ardmore Crest, Oldhaven, East Sussex, stepped into the confusion of the Golden Egg and tried to catch the attention of the landlord with a wave of his hand.

By the upheaval outside, Damien deduced that a carriage had overturned and that the occupants were trying to gather their wits and composure at the inn. An old gentleman wearing an outmoded wig and full-skirted coat haggled with the innkeeper about the price of renting another conveyance.

A gaggle of women gasped and moaned in shock by the fireplace, their fal-lals of fashion broken, smudged, and ripped.

"Can I help?" Damien asked as he finally caught the attention of the harried landlord.

That worthy of ample girth and red, sweating face shook his head. "No, all has been taken care of. No one was seriously injured. A collision between a gig and a traveling chaise. The coachman swears the horses were stung by a swarm of bees." He wiped the table by the door, the only table that didn't hold empty dishes and tankards. He indicated the chaos with a guilty smile. "My serving wenches ran orf with a troop o' soldiers wot stayed here last week, and me wife is busy in the kitchen. What can I do for you, sir?"

Damien laughed and sat down, stretching out his legs before him. "Bread and cheese, please, and a tankard of your best ale."

The landlord scuttled off, his face redder and creased with worry. Damien wished he'd stopped at a more quiet spot for sustenance, but he had to inquire at every inn along the road to London for the lost article.

Damn that millstone around his neck, his younger brother, Roger! Always in his cups, always landing in a scrape, one more serious than the last. He couldn't be trusted with a simple commission—as much was clear with this latest disaster. *If only I hadn't been called back to London, I would have made the contact myself.* But he couldn't very well avoid an order to avail himself to Lord Castlereagh at the Foreign Office.

Besides, picking up a delivery was child's play, something that Roger should have managed with ease even while inebriated.

Damien glanced around the room, noting that three of the ladies were young and comely. They simpered, blushing rose red when he smiled and nodded. Quite rascally of him to acknowledge them without an introduction, but hell, he *liked* teasing women as long as they kept a certain distance.

When they started wearing their hearts on their sleeves and insufferable longing in their eyes, he was quick to leave. An icy shudder went through him as he thought of emotional entanglement. He would not get caught in something

that would bring him a lifetime of pain. No, better stay with
the Cyprians and Opera dancers, who expected no more
than money and jewelry in return for their affection.

The landlord came from the kitchen bearing a tray with
the food he'd ordered. Damien drank deeply from the
tankard, slaking his thirst after riding out early from
London. The valise had to be retrieved before someone else
found it.

The din continued as more travelers entered in search of
a hot meal and a cold drink. As the landlord arranged the
food, Damien shouted over the noise, "Is there a piece of
luggage here, a valise, that a young gentleman left behind?"

The landlord cupped his ear to hear better, and Damien
repeated his question, his voice drowning in someone else's
neighing laugh.

"Your . . . what? Luggage?" the landlord asked, a confused expression on his face. He shook his head. "No."

Damien experienced the sinking feeling of defeat. "Very
well. See to your other guests." He turned to the food and
cut a slab of hard cheese to put on a slice of bread. Even the
simplest fare looked appetizing when the stomach rumbled
with hunger. He leaned back, chewing with relish.

Coming down the stairs, he noticed a set of dainty lady's
slippers and the fine material of a blue pelisse. A lady of
quality and her entourage, he thought as he viewed a maid
and two burly grooms carrying various boxes and parcels.
The young lady wore a poke bonnet, and Damien waited
eagerly for a peek at her face so carefully hidden by the
brims of the hat. *Brims so like horse blinders, so ridiculous,*
he thought with an inward snort. *Anything to protect a
lady's face from unwanted stares. . . .*

He saw a dark ringlet bouncing, and then the lady turned,
facing him.

He almost choked on his food as he recognized the
incomparable he'd fled from before he'd lost himself
completely in her sapphire blue eyes. Justine Bryerly. He
felt the familiar panic rising and the rapid thudding of his
heart. His chest squeezed with tension. He coughed, clearing his throat desperately and gulping down some ale. He

had not expected to see her for a long time, nor had he expected to react so violently to her presence.

She met his gaze and halted abruptly, her hand moving to her throat. He could have sworn he saw a dark shadow moving in her sparkling blue eyes, but as she noticed him, they filled with seething anger.

There was no heart behind that acid smile or she was hiding it well away from his probing stare. It was for the best really. Theirs had been a most uncontrollable tangle — one that should never have been. His heart thought otherwise, of course, that contrary devil.

He stood, giving a polite, if curt, nod. He had no desire to put the suggestion in her mind that he had followed her or that his decision had changed regarding their past relationship.

"Miss Bryerly," he said smoothly, keeping his inflection flat.

She dipped her head in haughty acknowledgement. "Lord Lewington." Her voice held a layer of ice. "Fancy meeting you here, milord."

"'Tis rather a surprise—"

"Certainly an unpleasant one," she filled in, her tone of voice now hoarse with frost. She turned away abruptly, but he had noticed the paleness creeping into her cheeks. "One that I could live without."

The landlord bowed deferentially as he spoke with Miss Bryerly. Damien could not hear the exchange—did not really want to hear it. He felt like running away but sat back down and continued with his simple meal. His heart had been shaken. Even his hands were trembling slightly.

The landlord walked with her toward the door, by him, and he overheard the last piece of their exchange.

"I had all your trunks and boxes loaded into your carriage, Miss Bryerly. All is in order. May I wish you Godspeed?"

"Thank you, Mr. Winnow. Your service has been most excellent."

Damien dropped a piece of cheese on the floor and bent to scoop it out of her way. She inadvertently stumbled against his shoulder, and he hastened to steady her, rising in the process. As he recalled from the past, she felt insubstantial yet so feminine against him. His arms remembered her all too well, and he looked down at her face, usually so full of life and animation. Her expression was dull now, or mayhap rather forbidding, lovely Cupid's bow lips pinched, and cheeks hollow, her eyes burning with dislike.

"Unhand me this instant!" she demanded. Her voice, akin to a bucket of ice water down his spine, washed over him.

He dropped his hands to his sides. "I only prevented you from taking a tumble, Miss Bryerly."

"You have no right to touch me. Get away from me!"

"If you think I tripped you on purpose to have an excuse to touch you, you're sadly mistaken."

"You have tripped me too many times as it is, and I beg of you to stay out of my way for the remainder of your life, and longer if possible."

He smiled at her murderous expression. "Really? You believe we might run into each other in the hereafter, in heaven?"

"Hardly that. I doubt that *you* will be going to heaven," she said, holding up her chin in challenge. "It suits me quite well—you in hell, and I in heaven."

He stiffened at her harsh words. "I hear you've taken it upon yourself to judge me—as if you alone have the Almighty's ear. I would like to point out—"

"I care not for your opinion, milord. With your actions, you showed me very clearly where we stand, and I don't know why I remain here talking to you at all."

His chest tightened as he looked into her accusing eyes. Something hard squeezed his heart, hurt him so that he found it difficult to breathe. Why could he not just let her go on her way and forget this insignificant interlude?

"Mayhap we haven't said everything that needs to be said to each other," he murmured, knowing it was true. To him at least. He had served their connection before all had been explored. He'd desperately wanted to sever their relationship . . . or at least he'd thought so at the time. He had panicked; he still was panicking.

She turned on her heel abruptly. "I have said all I want to say, milord. No reason to dally here. Good day."

He let her go. There was nothing more to discuss at the moment—nor in the future. He wondered what she was doing in Sussex, but it was not his business to find out, unless he made it his business.

He wished he hadn't laid eyes on Justine Bryerly here, raking up the past weeks in London. The memory of her would haunt his evenings, nag him in his sleep, and poke him as he woke up in the morning. He did not like to suffer, least of all because of a woman. Damn it all, he had no heart, everyone knew that! He was famous for it. Miss Bryerly was privy to it; she had always known.

Justine felt as if her world had tilted and she'd received a blow to her head. The wound in her heart she'd nursed until it had ceased to ache so fiercely had been torn open again. Too suddenly, too painfully. A deep sigh from the abyss of her feelings trembled on her lips, and she wished she'd never encountered the source of her misery. A malevolent imp of misfortune continued to rule her life, and she had no idea how to turn it away from her.

"All is ready." The coachman greeted her and helped her into the traveling chaise that was piled high with trunks and bandboxes.

"The sooner we leave, the better," she said, then sank down on the seat. "Keep a steady pace."

As the carriage left the inn yard, she caught a glimpse of the marquess leaning nonchalantly against the doorframe. He was still achingly handsome, a powerful male symmetry of broad shoulders, slim hips, and beautiful features. His Weston coat suited his tall form to perfection, and his striped waistcoat molded his strong torso.

His grin, in that lean bony face, was still as rakish as she remembered, and his lazy blue gaze still held that provocative glitter of interest, as if he could see into her heart, hold it, and caress it. *That's what rakes do best*, she reminded herself primly, *seduce with their demeanor*. Her fingertips could still remember the soft feel of his wavy black hair, and now she wished she'd never had the opportunity, or inclination, to touch him.

She was not going to lose her heart again, not to someone like the Marquess of Lewington.

With that resolution, she leaned back against the squabs and contemplated whether to stop for a midday meal or drive straight on to Milverly.

The day grew hotter as the sun climbed higher in the soft blue sky. At one o'clock they had reached the Downs, and Justine suggested to Agnes, sitting quietly in the corner, that they stop for a light meal and a glass of lemonade.

"I doubt we will be served anything but late supper in my sister's chaotic household," Justine added. "Nora was never one to concern herself much with the running of the household."

"But she is a sweet dear," Agnes said. "The house in Bath grew so quiet when she wed that good man, Lord Allenson, and moved away."

"Yes, Nora is spirited and full of mischief."

"Just like you then, Miss Justine," Agnes said with unusual familiarity. "You are two peas from the same pod."

Justine chuckled, realizing she hadn't really laughed for a long time. "I suppose that's the reason I argue with my sister a lot."

"You both want to be right—and prove that you are, in rather loud voices." Agnes's sunken cheeks grew pink, as if she finally realized that she'd spoken much too openly. She plucked at the silk fringe of her gray shawl. "I'm frightfully sorry, Miss Justine."

"But honest. You are right, you know, about me and my sister." Feeling better, Justine jumped down from the coach just as soon as it had halted at a posting inn on the outskirts of Lewes. She glanced around, seeing horses and other travelers. The air smelled sweet of cut hay and flowers, and the breeze lay soft upon her face.

With the changing scenery, she was slowly coming alive. It was as if the last weeks in London had been lived through a dream. This visit would be good for her, and since Nora was married, she might have some advice to give on matters of the heart.

Feeling lighter, she ran up the steps to the open door. As she stepped into the gloom of the taproom, she stopped to let her eyes adjust to the shadows that the light from the small windows could not dispel.

Guests were chatting and eating, cutlery clinking against pewter, and tankards scraping over the tables. Mostly locals, she deduced, but she glimpsed travelers in the private parlor beyond the stairs.

She stepped forward, trying to locate the innkeeper. She enjoyed stopping at spots like this where she could indulge in studying people from all walks of life. At home, or in London, her life was hemmed in by servants and carriages— and her relatives. Her mother would be shocked at her thoughts and her interest in common people.

"Well, well," someone she knew said in the shadows by the counter that held beer barrels and dirty glasses.

She stiffened as she recognized Lewington's deep voice. Was he following her? But he had been here before she arrived. Conceited that he was, he would think that *she* had followed him. That revelation brought wrath to life in her chest, a bright flame that rose in her throat and inspired angry words.

"What are *you* doing here?"

"Same as you, Miss Bryerly, visiting a public inn for a glass of refreshment. As far as I know, there's no rule against that," he drawled and then lifted a tankard of ale to his lips.

Her heart raced most uncomfortably, and she could not think of a suitable rejoinder. She gulped for air as she could not remove her gaze from his. Lewington's dark eyebrows rose a notch, and his eyes took on a derisive gleam.

"I have never known you to be speechless, Miss Bryerly."

"I have nothing more to say to you, as I told you in no uncertain terms. We concluded our discussion not three hours ago."

"Fate has put us together once more, and I have a strong

feeling we shall meet several times before this summer is over."

"Not if I can help it," she snapped, looking frantically for the landlord.

"I'm afraid he's not here to save you. He said he had to go out back and kill a chicken for supper."

She turned as if to leave, but he halted her progress with a hand on her arm. She looked at it and then into his eyes. "You can't seem to keep your hands to yourself, milord. I deeply resent—"

"Hmm, yes, I find it very difficult to—"

"That's enough! I did not come here to listen to your indelicate hints. Unhand me."

He obeyed. "I was only going to say the innkeeper's wife is more than willing to serve you." He called toward the back, and in a moment a plump woman wearing a brown gown, a white apron, and a mobcap on her curly hair, addressed Justine.

Justine knew she should let one of the grooms or Agnes order the food, but she did not have the patience to wait while they saw to the horses. "A pitcher of lemonade please, and something to eat. Served in a private parlor."

"A slice of cold meat pie and pudding, miss," the woman said briskly, "but I'm afraid the private parlors have all been bespoken."

Justine spied a table by the window and said she would eat there. Accompanied by Agnes, who had just entered, she left the marquess without another word. She sat down, and an inebriated farmer started speaking to her in familiar terms.

"A rare blessin' to rest me eyes on a pert li'l filly like yerself." He loomed over her, swaying lightly. As he laughed, his ale-soaked breath washed over her, and she recoiled.

Agnes pursed her lips in distaste and gave the uncouth man a baleful stare. "We are *not* seeking company."

The farmer balanced on one leg. "Wot if I am? I could use the soft bosom o' the lady to lay me weary 'ead upon."

Damien sauntered across the room and stood between the

women and the loud drunkard. Justine could only be grateful for his protection, even if his unwanted pursuit rankled.

"If you continue to molest the young lady, you shall find yourself in a brawl, and I shall draw your cork. I'm rather handy with my fives."

"A brawl. Naw, listen 'ere m'lord. I'm a peaceful man with a good eye for 'orseflesh and ladies' curvatures. No sin in that, is there?"

The marquess said nothing, and the farmer's leer faltered. He took a hurried step back, set down his tankard, and left.

Lewington turned toward her. "May I sit down?" he asked pleasantly as if he'd earned a reward. In a manner, he had.

"I don't think so." She shook her head, wondering if she ought to just leave the inn.

"This is not a suitable place for a gentlewoman traveling with only her maid for protection. I can offer my support for the time being."

Justine lifted her chin defiantly. "My grooms give me adequate protection, thank you."

He looked around the room. "Where are they?" Without waiting for an invitation, he sat down and put his tankard on the table. "You'll be safe with me."

"I'm not so sure about that," she said darkly, but she noticed that Agnes looked relieved.

"I am somewhat surprised at seeing you in these parts, Miss Bryerly."

She might as well tell him the truth, as he would find out sooner or later. "I'm on my way to visit my sister at Milverly."

He smiled, that melting roguish grin she both adored and loathed—because it was never hers alone. He gave it to any receptive female. "I say! We'll be neighbors this summer. How cozy."

Justine stiffened her shoulders. "I doubt we'll see much of each other. Rest assured, I will not seek your company, and I do not plan to attend the local assemblies in Oldhaven."

"How dull! Mayhap I can coax you to attend one of my

picnics. You cannot tie yourself to Nora's apron strings all summer."

"I might leave earlier than expected," she said icily. "Especially now that you've reminded me that we'll be neighbors."

He leaned closer to her, too close in her opinion, and his eyes looked decidedly wicked. "I thought you had planned to stay at Milverly in an effort to stay close to me."

"I'm not surprised that you would think that. You have never been able to look farther than your reflection in the mirror or past your own narrow thoughts." She continued before he could make a rejoinder. "You have always thought too highly of yourself, but mark my words, one day you will have hurt one too many people. You shall fall, and it will be a long fall from the precipice of your egoism."

His lean cheeks suffused with red, and she gloated over his discomfiture. *Serves him right!* she thought.

"Only a truly virtuous person like you has the right to judge others," he murmured, his voice pure ice.

The host returned to the taproom after his wife had placed food and drink before Justine and her maid.

"I think we will manage now without you hovering over us," Justine said to Damien in dismissing tones, "or are you hoping for a free meal?"

He gave her a dark, smoldering look but did not reply as the landlord approached their table and greeted them cheerfully. "I hope you find our simple fare to your satisfaction," he said, bowing deferentially.

Justine nodded and applied herself to the food with gusto. The landlord addressed Damien.

"I'm afraid that the article you're seeking was never found here, milord." He gave another bow. "I'm sorry I cannot be of more help."

Justine watched her erstwhile suitor, now adversary, from the corner of her eye. His lips drooped with annoyance, and his eyes glittered with frustration.

"Very well," he said with a sigh. "I daresay the valise is lost for good. A great inconvenience, alas."

Justine remembered the piece of luggage she'd found in

her room earlier in the morning, but angry that she was, she had no desire to inform his lordship of the fact. She knew it would be decent to tell him, but no explanation fell from her lips. She owed him nothing, only her scorn.

The unmitigated gall of him to suggest she'd visit Sussex just to be close to him! She ruthlessly suffocated the timid voice inside that suggested that his words had held a grain of truth.

She knew why the valise was so important to him, but she would not inform him that she had held the thousand pounds in her hand. As far as she knew, the valise still waited for its owner at the Golden Egg in Crawley.

Two

"YOU'RE VERY QUIET," Damien said, studying Justine's closed face. Frustration burned in his chest, mostly because of the missing valise, but also because of her, Justine. The memories of her—silky hair against his hands, soft lips so willingly pressed to his—were flooding back. He had thought he'd locked them in a dark corner of his mind, but a tidal wave of reminiscence came over him until he felt slightly dizzy. It worried him deeply that he'd failed to push the thoughts of her away.

"I was taught good manners—not to speak with a mouth full of food," she said as she set her fork aside. She glanced at her maid. "I think it is time to continue, Agnes. The company here has grown unbearably dull."

Anger fought with a desire to keep her at his side. For a lady of great beauty and compassion, she had a waspish tongue when she chose to apply it.

"I daresay you've tired of your own company, not mine, as we have not spent a great many minutes together," he said. He could tell he'd provoked her despite her show of calm demeanor. Even though he had no desire to argue with her, he found himself on a thorny path that he could not get off.

"One minute in your company is more than enough."

He smiled, but his heart sat like a painful knot in his chest. "I must carry a potent influence if one minute is all it takes to influence you."

She glared at him, those cool blue eyes now hot and blazing. "You haven't changed a bit! Always thinking of *you,* how *you* can impress, how *you* can turn the discussion back to *you.* Well! I'm appalled, sick and tired, and I did not ask for your company. Now kindly leave me alone."

Sorely provoked, he stretched his legs out before him, barring any escape route she might take. He should ignore her; it would be for the best, but somehow he could not capitulate. A devil he could not control rode him.

"Has it never occurred to you that *you* might be boring company," he said, not really meaning it. A rude thing to say, but she'd been rude to him.

She stiffened, her face darkening with distress as she searched his face for the truth. He closed her out with the implacable wall he was skilled at keeping up against unreasonable women.

"That is ample cause for this meeting to end," she said, her voice slightly choked.

He had to let her go; he had to forget her. He pulled in his legs. "I daresay you're right." He rose, bowed, and returned to the counter.

Crushing her feelings of inadequacy, Justine patted her mouth primly on a napkin and gathered her reticule and parasol. What Damien thought of her mattered not one whit! Agnes finished her meal hurriedly and went away to have a word with the grooms and settle with the innkeeper.

Justine forced herself to think about the future.

Mother would have swooned if she'd known that I didn't travel directly to Milverly, Justine thought, feeling a spurt of heady rebellion. No one was here to tell her what to do except the odious Marquess of Lewington, and he truly did not count. But if Father got wind of this, he would surely lock her up and never let her travel without her family again.

She would take advantage of her time of freedom, break

out of her despondency. Nora could not dog her footsteps until after the child was born. She waited by the door for Agnes.

"You look rather pleased with yourself," Damien, at the nearby counter, said and finished his ale.

"And why shouldn't I be? The weather is lovely, the food was plenty, and the lemonade cold. My only complaint is the company I've had to endure."

He barked a mirthless laugh. "I take it you're alluding to me, not the drunk farmer."

"If the shoe fits." She swung her parasol around, forcing him to move aside. With as cool a smile as she could muster, she walked past him and out into the sunshine. "Good day for the second time."

The sunlight glittered off a pond where three white ducks quacked and paddled. A black-and-white cat washed itself under the wide canopy of an elm, and a kitten frolicked nearby. *Bucolic paradise,* she thought. It ought to be easy to forget her heartbreak in the midst of this serenity. With a measure of luck and some cunning on her part, she would not have to set eyes on the Marquess of Lewington again.

Nora greeted her on the front steps of Milverly. She had greatly increased in size since Justine last saw her, and it was clear that the birth was close. Nora, taller than Justine and three years older, had the Bryerly coloring of black hair and blue eyes. The older sister sometimes took on the role of protector and mother. It had always been that way, but Justine chafed against the restrictions and the concern.

Nevertheless, Justine laughed with pleasure and hugged her sister, who wore a simple gown of canary yellow muslin and a wide straw hat on her head to protect her skin from the sun. Ringlets, so like Justine's, curled at the nape of her neck, but Nora had lost some of her youthful bloom owing to a difficult pregnancy.

"How are you?" Justine asked, noting the querulous slant of Nora's mouth.

"Hot and tired," Nora said with a grimace, "but now that you're here, all will be better. I just wish that Henry didn't have to spend so much time in London and abroad. State business, committee meetings."

"I shall endeavor to take the tedium from your life," Justine said and swung her five-year-old nephew, Edward, in the air.

"Auntie Justine, did you bring me a present?" he asked in a shrill voice.

Justine tousled his brown curls and looked at his round face and dark eyes gravely. "It depends, Eddie. If you promise not to put a mouse in my reticule—as you did last time—I might have a surprise for you."

"I promise not to put anything in your reticule, Auntie Justine, not even my favorite worm."

Justine shuddered and put him down. "Glad to hear it. In that case—"

Eddie lifted a glass jar filled with soil and held it toward her with one grimy hand. "Damien lives here."

"Damien?" Justine asked, laughter bubbling in her throat.

"Damien, the worm. I have a Roger, too, and a Henry, named after Father."

How absurd, Justine thought and then laughed out loud. "Very apt names." *As all gentlemen are worms at heart,* she silently told herself but then said, "He looks very comfortable."

Eddie pointed at a fat, singularly loathsome specimen. "I named this one for Damien. I heard a lady call him 'worm' once."

Nora cuffed him gently. "You should not listen to private conversations, Eddie. If your father finds out—"

"He won't, unless you tell him. Uncle Damien does not mind. He said it was a fine fat worm, and he was proud to have it named after him."

"I see." Justine felt that if she started laughing again, she would not be able to stop. "You call him Uncle Damien?"

"I see him sometimes when he comes for a visit. He said I could call him Uncle Damien since he wishes he were my uncle. He says his house is very empty without boys like me, but Father takes me there sometimes. Uncle Damien has the bestest horse—"

"That's enough, Eddie!" Nora sighed, rubbing her lower back and gave a rueful chuckle. "It's Uncle Damien did this, Uncle Damien did that, from morning till night. I'm afraid the marquess spoils Eddie terribly."

"I didn't know you had such close contact with your neighbor," Justine said, filled with misgivings. She went to retrieve a wrapped parcel from the carriage.

"Henry and Damien went to Oxford together; they have known each other for many years." Nora beckoned to the hovering footmen. "Bob and Harry, carry Miss Bryerly's trunks upstairs, to the green guest room."

She linked her arm with Justine's and they stepped through the hallway that was darkly paneled and gloomy but now brightened with armfuls of flowers.

The wooden floors gleamed with wax, and the whole house smelled like a meadow of wild flowers. Open windows let in the breeze from the sea, a tantalizing, salty freshness. *Nothing smelled as fresh as the sea,* Justine thought, remembering the foul odors of London.

She viewed the paintings on the walls in their heavy gilt frames, the plaster cartouches and garlands over the doors, and the murals on the walls above the stairs leading to the upper regions of the house. Angels and nymphs would always cavort on pink clouds until the paintings faded or the house was torn down. Tearing down Milverly—not likely. Milverly had been built in the sixteenth century, and leaded mullioned windows, flagstone floors, and rough ceiling beams were still visible in some of the rooms.

Part of the house had been rebuilt and brightened since those darker times of low ceilings, dark paneling, and stone fireplaces, but Justine liked the old rooms the best. They had a mysterious atmosphere, as if the kind spirits of long ago Allenson ancestors inhabited the very air. That aura disappeared from those parts of the house where renovations took place.

"I'm glad to be here," Justine said, inhaling deeply. And she meant it.

"I was afraid you would say no to my invitation. I like a

member of the family at my side until my time of confinement."

Justine felt closer to Nora that moment than she'd ever done before. Nora had never before *needed* her, the younger sister, the nuisance. "Let me take you upstairs to your bed, Nora. You look exhausted."

Nora did not protest, and slowly they made their way up the stairs to Nora's cozy bedchamber that had been decorated in amber silk wall panels and creamy taffeta curtains and bedhangings. The furniture was delicate French design, including a gilded bed in the cup shape of a scallop-edged shell.

Nora lay down on the chaise longue, and Justine swept an embroidered shawl over her sister's legs. Nora pulled her down to sit on the padded edge. "Now tell me the latest, tell me everything."

Justine swallowed hard, hesitant to bare her heart to her sister. "The latest gossip of the *ton?*"

"That, including your own offering to the gristmill. How did you get involved with Damien Trowbridge? I thought you knew that he's a rake—an incorrigible womanizer. I wouldn't allow him in this house if it weren't for Henry's fondness for the man. And truly, Damien has shown that he's not as vile as the rumors suggest. He's a quite decent man underneath the arrogant facade. I've come to quite like him since I moved here."

There she goes, prattling on, Justine thought. Saved from answering difficult questions, Justine was content to listen to the local gossip. It would spare her from Nora's prying for the time being.

"—so Damien invited the Wilsons, you know those infamous courtesans, and their entourage. For two weeks, this area relished the most salacious gossip, fed to us by the servants at Ardmore Crest. I suppose most of it is hearsay; you know how servants tend to exaggerate. Oh dear, is that the time?"

Nora glanced at the clock on the mantelpiece. "Soon time for supper. You should go to your room, you know where it is, and refresh yourself. We don't stand on formalities when only the family is at home. You can share a tray with me here, and Eddie shall join us for a short time before he goes to bed."

"Splendid," Justine said. She stood and smoothed down the shawl. "I won't be a minute."

Her room displayed the same gracile French furniture as in Nora's room, except for the bed, which was an ordinary four-poster with green silk hangings. The silk matched the wall panels and the curtains, and hints of green wandered among the flowers on the Persian carpet underfoot.

Agnes was unpacking and putting away the dresses in the clothespress. So many trunks—as if she were going to attend lots of gatherings, Justine thought, when in fact she'd come here to rest, entertain Nora, and perhaps ride along the sea.

She went to the open window and inhaled the fresh salty air. Above the swaying oaks and elms, she could see the wide blue span of the Channel. It held a glassy green tinge as the sun played over the waves.

From other visits, Justine knew that the village of Oldhaven had a secluded harbor, naturally carved by the sea between tall chalk cliffs. The inhabitants fished mostly for a living, and by the look of the hovels lining the harbor, it wasn't a very lucrative business.

"I'm almost finished, Miss Justine," Agnes said. "Everything has been emptied, but I don't know what to do with that valise. Fact is, I don't recognize it at all."

Valise? Justine looked at the alien piece of luggage on the floor. "What in the world! That's the valise I found at the inn! I gave it to Mr. Winnow for safe keeping."

"He must have forgotten about it and put it in among your things. After all, he was excessively busy that morning—so many travelers clamoring for his attention."

"Very well, I'll deal with it."

Agnes left the room and Justine hoisted the valise onto a chair. Damien had been searching all over for this. Was it his?

She opened it and saw the shirts and the neckcloths. No initials had been embroidered on the linen. She lifted them aside, finding the brown parcel at the bottom. Still there, just as it had been this morning. She held it in her hand. It was the size of a book, but much lighter.

Filled with curiosity anew, she unwrapped the package and stared at the roll of bank notes. Would Damien travel with such a sum and then forget the valise? He was not a wealthy man who could throw away a thousand pounds. *I would sleep with it under my pillow or chained to my leg so as not to forget,* she said to herself.

Justine viewed the inside of the brown wrapping paper and tried to read the strange symbols, numbers, and letters, thrown together haphazardly. She had no more success than on her previous try. They meant nothing to her, but mayhap this was a code for a horse race or some other betting event.

Damien had asked for the valise. He would know what the code meant, but she would not hand him the valise without knowing what made him so eager to locate it. She felt she had a right to know after he'd been so rude to her.

He'd stopped at the inns. He'd been searching for the valise, but why would he do that if *he* had left the valise behind? Wouldn't he know where he'd lost it?

Questions crowded in her mind, and she wished she had some answers. But she'd promised herself that she would stay away from Damien. And she would. She would keep her promise to herself, but there was no crime in snooping around for the truth, was there?

She quickly wrapped the money into the brown paper. Instead of putting it back into the valise, she buried it deep into her clothespress, behind her dresses. She sensed that without the package, the valise was worthless. If she sent the money back to Crawley every villain in town had a chance to steal it.

No, it would be safer in her wardrobe until she'd had a chance to discover the solution to the coded message. She was sure Damien could help her with that if he so chose, but she would keep her promise to avoid him. *She would!*

She returned to her sister's bedroom.

"You look lovely," Nora said and eased herself higher against the pillows.

Justine had put on a clean gown of cool green silk with a lace fichu around her neck. She'd brushed out her hair and wrapped it into a knot into which she'd stuck a green velvet flower.

"Mama's pearls would look good with that gown," Nora continued.

"I'm tired of Mama's insipid pearls," Justine said. "I can't wait to wear something more dashing. Sapphires, emeralds, opals . . ."

Nora laughed. "You always were in a hurry to grow up, find adventure, become a grand lady."

"I will wear Mama's pearls to the end of my days if I don't find someone to marry. To tell you the truth, Nora, I haven't found many gentlemen to my liking. The thought of spending a lifetime with one gentleman is frightening. What if—"

"You will marry the man to whom you give your heart," Nora said simply.

Justine paced the floor. "You loved Henry when you married him, didn't you?" she asked, agitated when reminded of her unsettled future.

"Yes very much. We have our disagreements, but Henry is a darling man. He treats me with respect, especially now that I'm enceinte. He's unassuming and supportive. I would not like a too demanding husband. I like to plod on without too much upheaval."

Justine thought about Nora's statement and realized she longed for passion, a heated relationship, mayhap even a demanding husband, who would sweep her away on an adventure of the heart. In that sense, she was different from Nora.

"I dislike the thought of marriage," Justine said, contrary to her previous thoughts of passion. She dared not think her dream would ever come true. "I don't have a desire for holy wedlock."

"You'll change your tune when the right gentleman comes to woo you. You need someone dependable and steady, not a rake and adventurer."

Justine wondered if Nora's mention of rakes hinted at

Damien. "Your description sounds utterly dull. I like a gentleman with more spirit."

"Spirit you have enough for two people. You might find Henry a dull dog, but he is the type who lasts and grows better with the years, like old wine."

"Perfect for you then," Justine said with a sigh. She sat down and waited listlessly for a sermon about responsibility and duty, but it never came. Nora only gave her an uncomfortable stare.

Two maids carried in trays laden with food. First there was a hearty vegetable and fish soup, then baked sole and peas, lamb, duck in aspic, and currant pudding.

Justine ate with good appetite. The fresh country air and the peaceful surroundings made her hungry, and Nora had a first-rate cook.

"I'm so glad you're here," Nora said, her blue eyes twinkling. "You have become a fashionable lady after only one season in London. I've heard that you took the capital by storm. You were called a diamond of the first water, an incomparable."

Justine laughed and set down her fork. "You're exaggerating, you truly are."

"My contacts in London never do," Nora said matter-of-factly. "Don't be modest. I wish I could have been there to share in your glory—to have brought you out myself, but in my condition, well, unfortunately I couldn't. I hear you had many admirers at your feet."

Now it comes, Nora will give me a sermon on Damien and my utter folly. "Only one suitor," Justine hastened to insert. "Lord Wyndham, a handsome and respectable man. But I did not love him. I know I made the right choice not to marry him. He's now happy with my old school friend Allegra Temple. I believe she's already in the family way—she hinted as much last time I saw her, right before traveling down here."

Nora did not speak. She chewed thoughtfully, then patted her mouth with a napkin. "At least you know your heart, Justine. So many debutantes are too inexperienced to know love from mere infatuation."

Justine sensed the gentle hint in those words and felt heat rise into her cheeks. She glanced away from her sister's probing stare. "What's new in these parts, Nora? Where are the swallows building nests this year, and are there herons in the estuary?"

Nora laughed. "I haven't had time to find out, but I know the local smugglers are very active at this time of year. We have some excellent French brandy in the cellars, as do most houses around here."

"Smugglers?" Justine remembered the valise, and her heartbeat raced at the thought of adventure.

"Yes. Or 'gentlemen' as they prefer to be called. Henry leaves a brandy order and money tucked in the window once a month, and the smugglers leave their wares on the back steps. We are supplied with tea also."

"Smuggling is illegal."

"Yes . . . but even the local justice of the peace, old Lord Hardwell, leaves his instructions late at night. No one has seen the smugglers, but I'm sure most of the local fishermen are involved. They hide their cargo and sell it around the country. If you want silks and French laces for a bargain—"

"You say you don't know anyone who is involved. Could one of the local gentry be actively participating?"

"You mean in the actual meeting of the French boats and transferring of the goods?"

Justine nodded. "Why not? It would be a great lark for the adventurous young blades."

Nora scoffed. "We don't have any young 'blades' around here, except Damien's younger brother, Roger Trowbridge. He's a wild one, just as Damien was at the same age. Damien calmed down when he took over the responsibility of the title after his father's death. Ardmore Crest is a very large estate and takes a lot of attention."

"He could still be a smuggler."

Nora pursed her lips in thought. "I don't know, but since he's involved in government business, I daresay he shuns illegal activities. Damien has contacts at the Foreign Office—or used to have during the wars with the French,

diplomacy and what not. He's a friend of Lord Castlereagh."
Nora threw up her hands. "Ah! Politics, how it tires me.
Now that Napoleon is a prisoner on St. Helena, we should
not have to fear a French invasion for a long time."

"Hmm, I thought Damien did nothing but gamble and
seduce society ladies," Justine said, confused by the different picture her sister was painting of the notorious rake.

"There is a quieter side to Damien, but I suppose he
amuses himself in London while spending time there—for
want of better things to do. At the Crest he's always
occupied with the estate. We invite him to dinner about once
a week when he's residing at the Crest. I'm sure he gets
lonely with only an old aunt for company. Roger spends
most of his time at university."

Justine cringed at the thought of having to share a meal
with him once a week while she visited Nora, but mayhap
he would decline the invitations owing to Nora's condition.
And, while I am here, he will not come around, Justine
thought. In London, it was he who had shunned her
company in the end, not the other way around.

"Roger is there now, so Damien has his hands full
keeping an eye on him and his wild friends."

"I have difficulty seeing Damien in the role of father,"
Justine said, thinking how deftly Nora had brought up the
subject Justine wanted to avoid at all costs.

"Eddie adores him. Damien will be a devoted father one
day."

"Damien is bound to teach his sons hazard and card
games right out of the cradle. I'm surprised you haven't
found a cup of dice in Eddie's room."

Nora shot her an impatient look. "You don't approve of
Damien, do you? But I suppose it's all for the best."

There it was at last, the first pointed question. "I'd rather
not talk about the marquess at all," Justine replied stiffly.
She finished her meal and gathered the empty dishes onto
the tray. "If you don't mind, I think I shall retire now. It has
been a long day."

Nora smiled and held out her arms for a hug. "Of course.
We have many more days to talk. I'm so glad you're here."

Justine wasn't sure she shared the sentiment at the moment, but her hug was genuine. She loved her sister, if not her inquisitiveness.

With the assistance of Partridge, her sister's maid, she helped Nora to settle for the night. As Justine went to her room, she realized she had something to do besides keeping her sister company and admiring the view of the sea from her bedroom window. She would make some discreet inquiries about the valise that had ended up in her possession by mistake.

Three

DAMIEN GOT OFF his horse and entered Ardmore Crest. He gave his hat and gloves to a footman by the door and told Struthers, the butler, that he desired a tray with cold cooked meats, bread, and brandy in the library.

Striding to the window, he looked at the sky. Three days hence would be the dark of the moon, the night the French luggers came to the English coast with their wares. He would have to find that valise and the code before it was too late to send the reply to their contact in France who received regular dispatches from St. Helena. Castlereagh knew when Bonaparte got up in the morning, what he ate, when he belched, and what time he went to bed. All through that one excellent spy in France, a royalist supporter.

Damn Roger to get involved with the smugglers on a lark! I should have known that Roger would bring disaster with him. I should have kept him away from the smugglers. Yet, Damien liked the company of his spirited brother, but it was unfortunate that confidential information would be jeopardized because of a young whippersnapper's mistakes. *Damn Roger for getting drunk during the mission.*

Damien kept cursing himself for trusting Roger with the errand. But there had been no one else to ask, as he'd hastened to attend a meeting at the Foreign Office.

Damien unbuttoned his blue coat and shrugged it off. He sat down behind his enormous desk laden with papers and stared listlessly at the vaulted ceiling. The air was hushed in the huge book-lined room, a peace he thoroughly enjoyed—except for the times when problems sought to disturb him. They often did, especially with Roger around the house.

He glanced with little interest at the estate ledgers stacked on his desk. The estate had been sadly neglected in his father's day, and it had taken years to straighten out the affairs of Ardmore Crest and its holdings. It had made him grow up, Damien reflected. The estate had been his salvation, in fact. It had given him purpose, a sense of self-worth he'd never had before. He'd been just like Roger, a fickle leaf in the wind, seeking pleasure after pleasure to dull the ache of living.

Roger bounded through the door, his velvet coat ripped and his neckcloth askew. Damien could smell the brandy fumes on his breath as he came up to the desk.

"Dammit, I bet a monkey on a cockfight in the next village and won. I bet on a large mean-looking bird with the sharpest talons I've ever seen, and he came through for me. Jack Umbleditch bet on the other cock and lost a hundred pounds."

Damien watched the flushed face and tousled brown hair of his younger brother. Roger had an open, freckled face and a sly grin that brought him many female conquests. Damien did not like the fevered look in Roger's blue eyes, but there was not much he could do to stop Roger's wild ways except for locking him in his bedchamber.

Roger would have to come out on the other side, find peace, find some real interest, some purpose in life. Only he could live through the hell of debauchery and find value in more subtle enjoyments.

All he could do, Damien mused, was to be there waiting, lending support. Act like a father, but so unlike their sire, who had done nothing but make sure to step on their self-esteem until they reached majority. But fortunately Father had died before Damien had been provoked far enough to kill him.

Damien clenched the edge of the desk until his fingers hurt. "I take it you celebrated your victory at the local tavern?"

"Yes, of course, I had to buy a round of ale for everyone involved. The locals expect it."

"What did you forget this time? Your watch, your horse?"

Roger groaned. "You didn't find the valise?"

Damien pushed back his heavy carved chair. "No, damn it, I didn't! I expect you to go out tomorrow and find it, even if you have to look in the ditches all the way to London. It was not at any of the inns where you stopped to wet your whistle."

"I'm sure I carried all the bags and packages from Crawley."

"All but the most important one. How could you be so careless as to get inebriated first thing in the morning? You should have known you'd get careless and forgetful!"

Roger hung his head, and two bright spots glowed in his cheeks. "Don't harangue me as if you're Father. I know I made a mistake."

"It was a mistake of gargantuan proportions."

"A thousand pounds for silks and brandy?" Roger gave Damien an incredulous stare. "You don't need the money. You have barrels of it. I don't understand why you're in such a high dudgeon about it."

No, you don't understand, Damien thought. He could not explain his poverty lest he reveal his own secret activities that helped to fill the Crest's coffers. "I expected you to deliver the goods, bring the money. Is that too much to expect?"

"You can give the smugglers their blasted thousand pounds without making a dent in your fortune."

It wouldn't make a dent, it would make a deep hole. You don't know the half of our difficulties. "That's not the issue. The point is, I trusted you to successfully negotiate the deal with the merchant in Crawley. You failed, and I cannot send you out again."

"Do your own dirty trade, Brother, but don't count on me to help you again." Roger gave him a dark look and stalked out of the room. He slammed the door, setting the glass fronts of the bookcases atremble. Another day had passed, and it had held its share of surprises.

"I'm not sure I want any more unpleasant shocks," Damien said, a sinking feeling filling his stomach. The ghost of Justine seemed to follow him around, nagging him, reminding him he'd left her, run away in a most ungentlemanly fashion.

She had expected more of him than he could give. He wished he could forget her — go on with life as he was used to, taking matters of the heart lightly, changing mistresses when it suited him.

Around noon the next day, Damien looked out the window, over the rolling park land and toward the sea. Here on the top of the hill, the panorama was breathtaking. Sunlight glittered on the waves, and a pinkish green mist hovered on the horizon. If it hadn't been for the smuggling, and the lucrative foreign contracts he'd negotiated for Castlereagh, Ardmore Crest would now have been sold or at least on the brink of ruin. This lovely view would always have been lost to him. He would have missed it more than he could say. He would have missed the familiar faces on the estate.

To his surprise, he'd discovered that he cared for the tenants, felt a responsibility for them he'd never expected. Their welfare was something to live for. If he failed now . . . it wouldn't bear thinking the thought to the end. What would his failure do to the people who depended on him?

Swearing under his breath, he decided to ride down to the village, then on to Fairhaven, a small hamlet on the westbound road. His latest mistress, Dulcie Jones, an Opera dancer of amazing agility, if less heart, was staying at a hostelry in Fairhaven, waiting for him.

The fishermen doffed their caps down by the Oldhaven harbor as he rode by. He'd known them all since he was a boy, and their sons and daughters now served at the Crest.

God forbid that anything should happen to take away their livelihood.

A brisk breeze from the sea bore the tang of seaweed and dead fish. The fishermen were mending nets for the next day's trip into the Channel for pilchards—the staple diet of most people in these parts.

Ben Bryman, one of the burly fishermen of his own generation, smiled and saluted. They had played together as boys. Ben was the leader of the smugglers, a fact that not all of the villagers knew. Damien was privy to the fact, as he more often than not stood beside Ben in the damp shale waiting for the French luggers in the dark of the moon.

"The pilchards will soon be running, milord!" Ben shouted over the screeching of the seagulls. "Isn't it grand?"

The secret code that all was going as planned. The French lugger was coming at the appointed time. "It's a grand day sure enough!" Damien shouted back.

The regular surge of the waves against the tide wall sounded soothing today, but sometimes the sea hissed and growled like an angry beast. He sat on his horse admiring the view of the harbor, slightly rounded in shape with an opening in the cliffs, beyond which lay the Channel. The River Noss wound through the hills down to the sea, creating an estuary beyond the village, a paradise for all kinds of seabirds.

Damien liked the birds, envied their freedom as they wheeled and floated effortlessly on the winds. Imagine spreading one's wings and rising up, up, up with the currents. *A miracle if there ever was one,* he thought with a sigh, and he set his heels into the sides of his horse. The gray trotted up the steeply sloping High Street, and he rode through the village and out on the main road. Twenty minutes later he entered the courtyard of the local inn, Fisherman's Luck, in Fairhaven.

He found Dulcie in the taproom drinking wine and tearing a loaf of white bread to pieces. She dipped a chunk into the wine and put it leisurely between her rouged lips. A smile followed as she caught sight of him. Her green eyes narrowed, and she tilted her head sideways, studying him.

"There ye are then, Damien. Never thought to see ye again."

He smiled, but instead of seeing her round face and soft seductive lips, he saw Justine's angry eyes and uncompromising jaw. Would the memories of her haunt him for the rest of his life?

He sat down next to Dulcie and put his arm around her shoulders. If anything, Dulcie would help him forget the ache in his heart. At least for the moment.

Justine spent the morning hours listening to her sister's prattle about village affairs. In the afternoon, she decided she needed a break from domestic issues and taking a ride would certainly serve that purpose. The day was clear and warm, and Henry kept excellent stables.

The groom, a surly old man named Bill Clark, saddled Nora's mare, Columbine, and gave Justine a hand up. She wondered if he was part of the group of local smugglers. In hopes of learning more, she said, "The wine served in these parts is excellent. I hear it's brought all the way from across the Channel."

He looked at her from under bushy black eyebrows, and she sensed he wasn't going to give her any information about the clandestine activities of Oldhaven. "I wouldn't know, miss, never drink the stuff."

"I see. You're partial to ale?"

He shook his head and ambled off. Frustrated, Justine headed for the path through the woods. It wound steeply up and then down toward the estuary.

On the other side of the river lived the man to whom she had once given her heart. She prayed Damien had never known and would never find out how much he'd meant to her. Never again would she be as foolishly taken in by a gentleman's smooth compliments and laughing eyes!

Admiring the view of the blue green water shimmering in the sun, she inhaled the sweet scent from the sea. The hurts she'd carried from London all at once seemed far away, and she could already feel the healing of nature filling her with

peace. She would live, and she would not be a fool again.
She had learned something.

As Justine greeted the vicar, who was standing outside the
old Norman church with its forbidding square tower and
tilting tombstones on the outskirts of the village, she slid out
of the saddle and held the horse's reins.

"How is your sister?" the vicar asked, his white hair
stirring in the sharp breeze. His eyes held a kind gleam.

"Getting nearer her time. I think she longs for it all to be
over," Justine replied, noticing the fresh paint on the church
door and the weed-free graves at the front. "Looks like
someone worked hard to refurbish the church and environs,"
she added.

The vicar nodded, his blue eyes glowing with pride.
"You're right. Lord Lewington donated a large sum of
money and set some of the young people in the village at
work here. He's making amends for the laxness of his
fath—" The clergyman's voice stopped abruptly as if he
were reluctant to slander the dead.

"Yes . . . it is kind of the marquess to care about the
villagers," Justine filled in, pleased to know that Damien did
not have a wholly evil heart.

Leading the horse, she continued up High Street to see if
anything had changed. She nodded to the people, and the
women, dressed in homespun gowns and kerchiefs, curt-
sied, smiling in the kind way she remembered. The children
gave her curious looks. The village of Oldhaven, built on
terraces in the hills, had not changed much since her last
visit and probably would not change much during her
lifetime, she mused.

She mounted Columbine, rode out of the village, and
chose the road west for an invigorating gallop. A while later,
she passed the gate leading to the inn at the outskirts of
Fairhaven. She glanced at the large gray horse tethered to a
pole outside. Beside it stood Damien, his face close to a
woman, whispering in her ear. Perhaps even kissing it. Their
tête-à-tête looked suspiciously intimate.

Dashed libertine! Justine sighed, as jealousy, like a dark,
insidious syrup, seemed to spread into her heart. She should

have known it was a mistake to ride anywhere. With her bad luck, she would encounter Damien. She rolled the reins tightly around her hand, wishing they were coiled around his neck. Ever since the moment she had met Damien, he'd given her nothing but grief.

Clearly there was more to come. It was her own fault to put herself in a situation where she might meet him, would have to endure his presence.

Drat it all! The decision to visit Nora had been a mistake, Justine thought as she hurried away from the disturbing sight of Damien so close to another woman.

She heard rapid movement behind her, knowing his horse would soon catch up with hers.

"I thought my eyes played tricks on me," Damien said as he arrived at her side, "but I see that my sight has not yet failed me."

She made her smile as frigid as she could. "You could always pretend not seeing me. I won't cry out in despair if you hasten to part from me without saying another word. A quick 'good-day' will suffice."

"I have to say I'm taken aback upon hearing how sharp your tongue has become since we parted in London."

"Who's to blame?" she asked tartly. With the hope of getting rid of him, she pulled in the reins on the road going past the cottages and down to the sea. She slid out of the saddle and moved onto a narrow footpath where he had difficulty following her. But now also on foot, he pursued her.

"Are you blaming *me* for your ill humor?" He smiled incredulously.

"I certainly do not inspire ill humor in myself. I make an effort to stay cheerful, so someone has to take the blame."

She wished he didn't look so handsome when his face creased in laughter. Why did he have to look more like a charming god than a regular fellow whom she could more easily forget? Why did her heart have to flutter like a mad butterfly every time she caught sight of him? And why was he in such a good mood?

"Very well," he said with a theatrical sigh. "I guess it is

the gentlemanly thing to do to take the blame upon my shoulders. If it makes you feel better—easier at heart."

"Your absence would improve my temper miraculously," she said, walking faster and faster.

"Can we bury our mutual animosity for a moment, Miss Bryerly?" he asked, easily keeping up with her stride.

She could not find it in her to discard her anger. "I see no reason to speak further."

"As long as you stay in Oldhaven, we will meet occasionally. There's no reason why we have to argue every minute."

"I have no intention of seeing you again." Justine's chest started to ache with the exertion of walking uphill. If there had been any sign of a mounting block, she would have used it to get onto her horse and trot away. She wished he didn't lead his mount so close to her sweaty mare, and Lewington crowded her with his presence and his heady virile scent. All she wanted was to forget that she'd ever known the dratted man!

"Whatever your intentions, Miss Bryerly, fate has a way of ruining them."

She halted, now exceedingly angry. "I don't understand why you have to torture me with your unwanted presence! Why did you follow me just now? I did not ask for it."

He stood so close she could see the faint lines around his eyes, the strong jaw that she remembered how it felt to touch, and his deep, shadowy eyes. "Yes . . . I know. I appreciate your willingness to speak frankly. I only followed you to ask about Nora. How is she?"

His words deflated Justine's bubble of wrath. She hadn't remembered his friendship with Nora and Henry. Once again, she felt she had made a fool of herself. She quickly glanced away and took a deep, steadying breath. "Nora is as well as can be expected under the circumstances."

"The waiting must chafe on her nerves."

Justine panicked. His voice softened as if he sensed her mortification. "The doctor said she has to rest until her time comes."

Silence fell between them, a silence filled with suggestion

and unspoken questions. He trapped her gaze, and she had to suppress her urge to flee.

"You would be a good mother, Miss Bryerly."

"You don't know me well enough to speak in such a familiar manner," she said stiffly.

His voice lowered a notch. "I know you well enough to remember that you're a child at heart. You enjoy simple pleasures—just like a child."

"If you're implying that I am as easy to fool as an infant, you may keep silent."

"You carry more spines than a hedgehog, Miss Bryerly."

"They serve me well in situations like these." She continued walking and came upon a tavern. To her relief, there was a mounting block next to a nearby stable. She led Columbine over the cobbles and stepped up onto the block. "And now, since your curiosity about my sister has been stilled, I say my *adieu*."

"Give my regards to Eddie and my namesake, the worm."

"Don't expect me to run your errands."

He gave her a mocking bow, his face a mask of politeness. Damien's character held many layers, and she realized she hadn't known more than the most superficial ones in London. The thought of knowing more about him disturbed her no end. No, no, it would never come to pass, she thought.

She dug her heels into Columbine, relieved to leave Damien and his secrets behind. And his mistress. She wished she could have riled him about her, but a lady did not speak of the *demi-monde*.

Four

ANOTHER DAY PASSED, and Justine could not force her thoughts away from the Marquess of Lewington's indolent blue eyes and wicked grin. *Drat him, and all gentlemen with charming smiles! They should all be carted off to Botany Bay on a convict ship. . . . Surely it should be illegal to seduce young ladies with winks and roguish grins.*

From one of the salons on the second floor at Milverly, she had a clear view of Ardmore Crest upon the hill, a dowager of a house with its great dignity and august years. He lived in that mansion, his thoughts filling the atmosphere and his laughter tickling the ears of the young serving girls.

Ancient oaks and elms protected the venerable home of the Trowbridge family, and the park had the groomed look that could only have been created by dedicated gardeners. Sometimes she wished she had a telescope, then hated herself for her base instincts to spy on him.

"I have a note from Clara Trowbridge, Damien's aunt," Nora said at the breakfast table. "She's most deaf, the old dear, and she's eager for female company. She knows I'm not strong enough to attend, but she has invited you to a small dinner party. One of Damien's female relatives, Imperia Dunmore, and her companion, Monique de Vauban, will collect you in the Dunmore chaise. Lady Dunmore lives in a neighboring village."

"No! I won't accept the invitation," Justine said, smoothing the skirt of her striped muslin gown. "I have no intention of visiting the Trowbridges in your place. When the child is born, you may take up the threads of your friendships once more."

"If you're afraid of encountering . . . Damien, have no fear. This is a gathering for females only. Clara has her own apartment at the Crest. She does not entertain Damien's friends as a rule, for she does not approve of his 'wild' ways." Nora laughed. "I believe she doesn't realize that Damien has grown up. He's no longer a wild young blade like his brother, Roger."

Justine remembered the valise, still trying to make up her mind what to do with it. She had no desire to approach Damien and confess that she had it among her things.

Just the thought of speaking with Damien chilled her blood. But she would have to do something about the valise. It went against her principle of honesty to conceal a lost item from its true owner.

Mayhap she could bring it to the dinner party and leave it in the house somewhere. . . .

"You're not listening to a word I've said, Justine!"

"I'm sorry. I was indulging in some wool-gathering."

Nora gave her an impatient stare. "I said it would please me greatly if you would attend in my place. Clara is a dear, and rather lonely in that old rambling house with only the servants for company. The gentlemen have their own interests and business, and they do not include Clara very often."

"She has probably chosen to stay away from their company, and I don't blame her," Justine said under her breath. Nora was growing quick-tempered as her time came closer, and Justine felt she had to smooth her sister's ruffled feathers. Anything to get through to the end. After the child was born, Justine would travel home to Bath. Until then, she would have to endure Nora's flights of fancy and bouts of hot temper.

"Even though it's most proper for you to wear white, you may wear my lovely emerald green silk gown and a Norwich shawl. And I shall lend you my emerald earrings for the evening."

Thus bribed with silk and gems, Justine could not argue further. She despised herself for her weakness but knew she was secretly eager to see the inside of the Lewington estate.

Two evenings later, she found herself escorted to the dignified doorstep of Ardmore Crest by Lady Imperia Dunmore, a woman of ample proportions and an ample voice that would not cease often to draw breath. At her side waited a mousy young woman who must be Mademoiselle de Vauban. She nodded in greeting as Justine spoke of the weather, but the conversation lagged before they had a chance to discuss other matters. Mademoiselle de Vauban's skin had the unhealthy pallor of someone who rarely ventured outdoors. Lady Dunmore probably kept a tight rein on her companion, Justine thought.

Candles glinted in the windows, welcoming the guests. The evening was dark, heavy clouds hanging on the horizon, bringing dense humidity and a promise of rain.

As a footman let down the step of the carriage, Justine thought she saw a shadow flit past a window by the front door.

A man? She must have been mistaken. *Who would lurk in the shadows of Ardmore Crest? The servants kept an eye open for intruders, surely. Probably one of the outdoor servants.*

The butler greeted them in the hallway and took their evening wraps.

"You look lovely, Miss Bryerly, though I'd say white would be—oh, well, I daresay emerald green is a good enough color," Imperia Dunmore commented, while studying Justine through her quizzing-glass. Her gray eye was hideously enlarged, and Justine suppressed a sudden urge to giggle. She hadn't giggled much lately. She had used to laugh a lot with Allegra Temple at the young ladies' academy.

"Thank you," she said. *I wish I could say the same about you,* she added silently to the matron wearing a leaf green ill-fitting gown trimmed with bands of rust, and a towering purple turban with three bobbing ostrich feathers. The tight fit of Miss Dunmore's bodice over a large bosom made Justine worry about ripping seams and escaping flesh.

A set of garishly set rubies circled the wrinkled neck, and Justine swore silently she would not wear anything that vulgar when her skin could not longer set off the stones. She hoped she could remember that vow in thirty years' time.

Nora had lied, Justine thought immediately as the butler ushered them into the drawing room where a footman in a powdered wig and Lewington livery offered a glass of wine.

Gentlemen *were* present at this gathering for ladies only. Anger flared through Justine at her sister's deception. Why did Nora have to meddle in her life? Did she think she could bring her and Lewington back together? The marquess and a younger man stood by the fireplace wearing biscuit-pale pantaloons and evening coats of black velvet.

She had to curb the urge to turn on her heel and leave. Readying herself for battle, she set her lips and straightened her back.

"Miss Bryerly!" said a slim elderly lady in a booming voice that belied her narrow form. Clara Trowbridge walked toward her with outstretched hands. "I'm so glad you could come," she added in that voice much too big for her body. "I've heard so much about you." Justine remembered that people who were hard of hearing often spoke too loudly.

"Nora sends her regards."

"I miss her cheerful company." Miss Trowbridge looked at Justine with kind, twinkling blue eyes. Her skin held a map of wrinkles, and her hands were cool and papery to the touch. She pulled Justine with her. "You must meet my nephews, Damien and young Roger."

Taken aback, Justine wondered if Damien had never mentioned her to his relatives. The thought that she'd meant so little to him while he'd meant so much to her during those weeks in London rankled.

Damien bowed over her hand, holding her fingertips. A

warm sensation curled up her arm, and she snatched her hand back. "We meet again—unexpectedly," he said smoothly. "How delightful."

"It certainly was unexpected to me," she said, cursing the heat rising in her cheeks.

"And this young rapscallion is Roger," Miss Trowbridge boomed. "He has given me many gray hairs."

"Aunt Clara, it is monstrously unfair to slander me to strangers." Roger had brown eyes and Damien's devilish grin. His shorter athletic build pleased the female eye, Justine thought, and the dark rings around his eyes might intrigue a less experienced lady, but not her. Self-indulgence with the bottle and late nights brought about such smudges of dissipation.

"But mostly true," Damien drawled, "except for the gray hairs I gave her."

Aunt Clara stilled, her eyes riveted to his lips. *She is surprised at his words, as if she didn't expect him to say something so revealing about himself,* Justine thought.

"I hope I no longer do," he added in an undertone.

"I'm surprised you would admit to a less than perfect past, Lord Lewington," Justine said sotto voce.

Miss Trowbridge had evidently read the words on his lips. She fluttered aside, waving a hand as if the question was too confronting to warrant an answer. "Come, Miss Bryerly, you must tell me all about Nora and her current . . . state." She pulled Justine with her.

"She would welcome a visit to ease her tedium."

"Yes, I shall drive over." Miss Trowbridge threw a glance at the young Frenchwoman, a gray shadow behind her formidable employer. "Mayhap I could convince Mademoiselle de Vauban to accompany me. She's having a difficult time, the poor dear. So lonely. Her father, the Comte de Chambeau, took his family out of Paris in a hay cart at the height of the Terror. Monique is the only survivor—she says. She's completely cut off from her past. There were nasty rumors, though, that her older brother chose to side with the revolutionaries. He can't have been more than a young boy at the time. I would think he's dead now."

"But why is she living with Lady Dunmore?" Justine could not help but ask. "They seem somewhat—well—mismatched."

"You see, Lady Dunmore's aunt was married to one of Monique's uncles—a Scotsman. I think Imperia felt it her duty to take care of the orphaned child." Miss Trowbridge heaved her thin shoulders. "I would have done the same under the circumstances."

Damien came closer, and the old woman changed the subject. "We shall certainly call on Nora to ease her tedium."

"Does that include gentlemen callers?" Damien asked, his eyes hooded in the flickering candlelight.

"It depends if they are friend or foe," Justine said coolly. She wished she hadn't come here and told herself that this was the last time she would let Nora manipulate her into an undesirable position.

"I'm sure she still considers me a friend," he said with that maddening smile.

"More the fool she," Justine said in a low voice.

He pulled her subtly aside. "She considers me a friend, so why should I allow your venom to keep me away from Milverly?"

Justine took a deep breath to steady the tumult inside her. "If Nora knew the whole, she would be the first to send you packing. She would ask you never to return."

His gaze held an edge of frost. "What have I done now? Anyway, Nora was never petty and narrow-minded, like—"

"—like me?" she filled in, resenting his hinted slur upon her character.

"Do not put words into my mouth, Miss Bryerly. I must say I am wholly out of patience with you. There is no need to draw daggers every time we meet."

"Preferably, we should not meet at all." She walked away, joining Miss Trowbridge, who was speaking with Imperia Dunmore about stale tea cakes and fugitive pastry chefs.

Justine addressed Mademoiselle de Vauban. "I hear you're an excellent needlewoman," she said, hoping the assumption would be true.

"Thank you, I do enjoy my embroidery," the French-woman said with a slight accent. She smiled, but at the same time her dark eyes probed the depths of Justine's mind as if trying to read her thoughts. Justine doubted that Mademoiselle de Vauban missed anything going on around her, despite her retiring demeanor. "I am currently embroidering new chair covers for Lady Dunmore, a floral pattern of my own design."

"For Lady Dunmore? Such an undertaking, especially since the chairs are not your own."

The mademoiselle lowered her long curling eyelashes to hide the expression in her eyes. "Lady Dunmore has been very kind to me." She shot furtive glances at Roger and Damien. "I daresay she expects me to give something in return for her generosity."

"I would think she would feel it her duty to find a suitable husband," Justine said as she noticed the quick glances at the gentlemen.

"Oh, no," the mademoiselle said, fluttering her hand in agitation. "I cannot expect anything like that. Lady Dunmore needs me, and I—I like to think that I am close to France." She sighed. "I look out to sea and imagine France on the other side. Sometimes, when the skies are clear, I think I can see my homeland."

"You must miss it very much."

Mademoiselle de Vauban's head drooped on her slender neck. "*Oui*, I sometimes feel a great longing to be gone from here. But I have no one."

Justine forgot the gist of her conversation with Miss Trowbridge. "I hear you might have a brother. . . ." Too late did she realize her faux pas.

The Frenchwoman flinched as if slapped, and her face took on a masklike stiffness. "I have no brother," she said coldly. Her hands plucked at the humble lace edge at her throat. "Well . . . I am not supposed to acknowledge my brother."

"I'm so sorry," Justine said, knowing that the mademoi-selle would not easily forgive her for listening to gossip about the past. "I did not intend to pry into your life."

Mademoiselle de Vauban lifted her chin. "I daresay my name is connected to scandal, but I am proud of my brother for standing by his ideals."

The conversation held a promise of intrigue, but the discussion came to an abrupt halt as the butler announced that dinner had been served in the dining room. Justine slanted a glance at the marquess, noting that he'd turned the company his back and was staring out the window, a wine glass in his hand.

Damien saw that the rain had let up at last. The night was perfect for the smuggling vessel to rendezvous with the gentlemen waiting on the beach with pony trains and wagons to haul away the wares.

He longed to leave this oppressive drawing room and ride down to the hidden cove where the landing was taking place, but his absence would have been questioned. He had to obey Aunt Clara's command the few times she asked for his presence at one of her small gatherings.

It was unfortunate that she'd invited Justine Bryerly, but something had stirred in his chest when he saw her in that green silk gown and her gleaming black hair, curled and bound up with velvet ribbons.

He had denied the feelings that tried to grip him in the past, but the past had caught up with him, dredging up the old fears, the memories of his childhood. He knew the time had come to face them, but it still made him reluctant to bring the anger, the disappointments, the disgust, to the surface.

He didn't want to hurt anyone, least of all Justine Bryerly, whom he could not forget. Running away from her had not helped, and now fate confronted him at every corner. He drew a deep breath as he finally admitted to himself that he'd run away from his feelings and from her, the woman who stirred his deepest longings. He'd run into a wall. He could never flee from himself. Or her.

Clara had seated him next to Justine. He had expected as much. Clara—always hoping he would marry and settle down, give her children who would fill Ardmore Crest with laughter—put him beside any eligible female she could lure to the Crest.

"Have some more fish soup, dear," Clara said to him, her eyes wise, as if she could read his inner turmoil. "Made from haddock caught this morning."

He smiled and complied, not really tasting the fragrant soup. The fishermen caught fish in the morning and brandy casks at night.

As if echoing his thoughts, Justine said to Miss Trowbridge, "Nora told me about the local smugglers. They leave brandy and tea on the back steps once a month. Do you know about that?"

"That's right, but we don't speak much about it locally. Illegal business, you know, and best left alone." Miss Trowbridge patted her mouth on a napkin and waved to the footmen to bring in platters of cold salmon.

"But still, the smuggling is generally condoned?" Justine continued.

"The excise is outrageous on the wares crossing the Channel. If the tax were reasonable, there would be no need for smuggling," Roger explained, his eye eager on the bottle of claret on the sideboard.

"If I wore a gown of smuggled silk, I would worry that someone might recognize the material."

"There's no fear of that, surely," said Miss Trowbridge with a laugh.

"Not everyone is as conscientious as you are, Miss Bryerly," Damien said, letting his gaze linger on her lovely face. Her blue eyes blazed at him, a message of defiance.

"I'm sure *you* do not mind drinking smuggled brandy," she said in an undertone that only he could hear.

"I've been known to imbibe a glass or two," he said nonchalantly.

She raised her voice. "I hear that smuggling can be quite profitable as well."

"It's a dangerous business," Roger said. "If the smugglers are caught, they're most likely to hang. The locals would not be willing to take such risks without getting a great reward."

Damien gave her a thorough scrutiny, sensing hidden layers to her statement—all based on her tone of voice, as if she knew more than she was willing to share. But he had no desire to go into the topic of smuggling, not when he was part of the group that made business with the French. Besides smuggling, he had another, more important, business across the water.

Justine watched Damien surreptitiously throughout dinner, until the last spoonful of strawberry ices had been savored. He assisted his elderly aunt to the drawing room. *Always the perfect charmer,* Justine thought, her mind tainted with distrust. Before the door closed to the drawing room, she saw that he did not rejoin his brother at the dining table for port, but headed out the front door.

Consumed by curiosity, she said to Clara that she needed to freshen up and left the room. Footmen stood motionless in the hallway, but as far as she could tell, they did not see her sneaking into the library and out onto the terrace.

The night wore a heavy cape of darkness. Warm humid air closed around her, bringing summer scents of honeysuckle and wild roses to her nose. She'd been a fool to think she could spy on Damien. Why would she *want to* spy on him at all?

She suspected the valise played an important role in his life. A secret life she knew very little about. *Obsession,* she thought. She felt this wild need to know more about him, to learn his every secret before he discovered her investigation into his secrets.

That's why she hadn't yet revealed the whereabouts of the valise to him. She had to discover what Damien was hiding. Somewhat hazily she realized she wanted to get back at him for hurting her in the past. *Revenge.* Shying away from that unpleasant revelation, she hurried the length of the terrace.

The park lay before her, the darker masses of trees and shrubs taking on threatening proportions in the darkness. She thought she heard voices as she came around the corner of the mansion, but only silence met her and the rustle of some nocturnal animal. Mice! Or something even larger . . .

Shuddering in disgust, she almost ran back inside. She finally managed to collect her nerves. If she acted faint-heartedly, she would never learn anything about Damien.

Following the long drive leading down to the gatehouse at the bottom, she thought she saw the flicker of a lantern out on the road. She stumbled in her thin slippers but managed to reach the gate before the light had disappeared. It bobbed along a path in the woods on the other side of the road.

Not thinking of her own safety, she followed where her curiosity led her.

Having staggered along on the uneven path, she came upon two men speaking in a clearing. She took shelter behind a tree, but not really close enough to overhear their conversation. Disjointed words floated on the wind.

"Had . . . more. Message . . . what happened. Lost . . . tell Jacques . . . another time."

She recognized Damien's voice. The other man had the sturdy build of a laborer. Mayhap a fisherman or a local farmer. But why would the Marquess of Lewington involve a laborer in a whispered conversation in the woods?

She could barely contain her curiosity, but if she stepped any closer, they might discover her.

"Milord . . . triple casks . . . cargo . . . ," the other man said hoarsely.

Damien straightened up, looking away from the lantern. He seemed to sniff the air as if it would give him the answers, as if he could sense her. A soft breeze soughed through the branches overhead.

He spoke a notch louder. "Very well, do it. I'm sure we'll be able to sell the extra casks for a tidy profit. Your children shall not go hungry this winter."

The other man bowed. "Bless you, milord."

Justine blinked. The man had disappeared, melted into the darkness very quickly, and with him the lantern. She had to run back to the house before Damien discovered her.

Without waiting to see what Damien's next move would

be, she hurried back up the path and ran the length of the drive. When she reached the terrace, her side ached and her breath came in tortured gasps.

She couldn't very well step through the front doorway. The footmen would have noticed her disheveled state. Slipping into the library, she straightened her hair and gown. Miss Trowbridge must wonder what had happened to her. With her hand on the door handle, she was ready to return.

"Miss Bryerly? Are you seeking my company?" Damien drawled behind her.

She stiffened. Slowly turning around, she stared at him defiantly. He stepped into the room through the open terrace door, no worse for wear after a trip to the woods. She hadn't looked in a mirror; she might have twigs in her hair and leaves in her sash.

"I mistook the room. I'm looking for a place to refresh myself."

His gaze raked her from head to toe, and heat rose into her cheeks at his scrutiny. "As you can see, this is the library. You look like you fell into the holly shrub below the terrace," he said, his voice implying he didn't believe her. "What happened?"

She took a deep breath and met his prying gaze directly. "Nothing happened, but I could always count on you to point out my flaws. It is an uncouth and ungentlemanly habit."

"Well, I've been called a rake, and surely rude remarks are the normal expressions of rakes. Don't take it personally." He leaned against the doorframe, his lips quirking upward. "In fact, I think you look rather charming with your hair is disarray and twigs adorning your dress. If I didn't know better, I'd say you just kept a secret tryst in my garden. But I do know better, so you can take that frown off your face. Besides, the only eligible gentleman except myself is Roger, and I believe he's keeping his appointment with the brandy bottle."

"Since you have explained why I would never keep a secret tryst with your gardener or Roger, I have a right to know your part in the goings-on. What were *you* doing outside in the dark?"

"A rendezvous with a paramour would not be beyond me—as you well know. You and I met any number of times without your chaperone ever being the wiser."

"How you twist my words around!" She balled her hands into fists. "I do regret meeting you clandestinely in London, but fool that I was, I believed your interest was honorable. But no, you ran away, left me without a word, just as soon as you had me swooning at your feet. Tell me, did I have stars in my eyes? What stopped you from completely ruining me?"

He walked toward her, his blue eyes dark with frustration, and something else—aggravation? Maybe even passion . . . "As a rule, I don't compromise ladies. Some father might feel compelled to call me out and shoot me through the heart. I have more of a sense of self-preservation than that, and I am too young to die."

"Always thinking of yourself." Bitterness welled up in her, tainting all the warm feelings she'd had for him, and still had.

"No one else will do it for me," he said in a muffled voice.

"You're wrong! I would have given my all, my very life for you once. Very foolish and childish of me, of course, but I believed in love."

She shouldn't be talking to him about their past, touching that sore spot that had never quite healed. She had sworn she would never let him get an inch of her again or see the pain he'd inflicted.

He stood so very close, his eyes alert, his gaze arrested as if someone had given him a punch in the stomach.

"You would have given me that?" he asked, his voice hoarse with disbelief.

She instantly regretted having said those words. "Not any more, of course. It was the ravings of a much more innocent girl. You made me leave my childhood behind, and for that I will always be grateful. I shan't make the same mistake with other gentlemen in the future."

She knew she should leave, but she couldn't find the strength to turn around and head for the door. She stared into his hypnotic eyes, unable to shake off the web of enchantment weaving around them. A rake and a smuggler, possibly a spy, she reminded herself. A criminal and a man who used women to satiate his dark desires.

She kept telling herself those words over and over, but she couldn't fight him when he swept her into his arms and kissed her.

His mouth roved hungrily over hers, plunging, plundering, as if he'd never kissed her before, and she felt as if she'd never been kissed before—not like this—even though his mouth had caught hers intimately in the past.

He groaned and held her tighter, his hands hard on her back, his chest an unyielding wall against her.

Struggle! she thought frantically, but she wanted no more than to be held, swept up by his passion.

He slowly lifted his face from hers, and she gazed into his eyes. They burned her, dark with passion and a feeling she could not name, but she kept staring at him.

"Why did you leave me in London without an explanation?" she whispered at last, when she could find her voice. "You owe me an explanation."

He gently released his overpowering embrace, setting her away from him. He moved to the opposite side of the room and dragged his hands through his hair. Hanging his head, he looked at the stacks of paper on his desk.

He spoke at last, his voice hitched on deep emotion, "I was terribly afraid of my own feelings, Justine. They were like an abyss into which I dared not look."

"Afraid?" She listened, waited frantically for more, but he remained silent, his back turned toward her. "How am I to believe such a statement, Damien? It's the kind of suggestive words you say to a lovesick girl to get her sympathy, to get your way with her."

"It's the truth, I swear it!" He turned, his face pale, his gaze savage with sudden anger, as he evidently could sense her distrust.

"Damien, I don't know what is true any more. You've always been so eloquent with the ladies, so in control."

"Just a game——"

"Really?" Feeling suffocated by her own doubts, she said, "I have to leave now. This is yet another situation set for disaster."

"What else do you want me to say or——do? Fall to my knees in humility? In London, I felt that our love should not be, as I would never be able to respond with your depth of feeling. I had so little to give as I could not believe in a future with you. I had to leave. It was cowardly to abandon you without an explanation, but the depth of my feelings for you truly terrified me. I never thought love was *possible;* I believed that it was destined to fail."

"Balderdash! You could have stayed and discovered your heart. You did not have to run away. You could have trusted me."

"I have learned so much since we parted, learned that——" he said, letting the rest of the sentence fall away. "Oh, God——how——"

"I learned something, too. Don't trust rakes with glib tongues. I've had enough of this useless conversation." She made sure her hair was pinned up and her gown straight. His kiss still burned on her lips, and she fought a wild urge to cry. She could still feel the imprint of his strong arms on her back, but that drove her to the door as fast as her legs could carry her. Every part of him signaled danger and destruction, and she fled without giving him another glance.

"Don't go," he called out in a hoarse voice. "You were the one who wanted an explanation."

No, she could not believe him——dared not. What if he had only fabricated the explanation to play on her sympathy? If she wanted to keep her sanity, she had to put as much distance between them as she could. *So help me God, I will never fall for his seductive caresses and smooth phrases again.*

Five

DAMIEN REMEMBERED HER kiss. He had tasted many, some seductive, some sultry, some even unpleasant, but a kiss had never intoxicated him like Justine's. The pure, sweet delight of Justine Bryerly might bring down his carefully constructed, *safe* world if he wasn't cautious.

She made him vulnerable, and he would become like the sniveling boy who'd been forced to witness his father's cruelty toward the whores he'd brought home. He would feel the rage, the helplessness all over again as he'd been unable to help them away from degradation.

He could not afford to show any emotional weakness to the females he met, not now, not ever. He could not live with their disdain, their scorn, should they find out that he had a weak spot in his heart, because ultimately they would turn against him, as had the women who turned against his father. They had hated him.

Love that lasted simply did not exist.

Damien loathed weakness. Sleepless, he paced the Oriental carpet in the library and slammed his fist on the top of his polished desk so that the quill fell out of its silver stand. He had planned his life meticulously, and on the outside, the Trowbridge family thrived—if just, but he realized he could not expect his emotions to run the smooth track of a business venture.

The whole tower was crumbling around him thanks to Miss Justine Bryerly, the incomparable Miss Bryerly, the kissing Miss Bryerly.

"Damn her to hell!" he said aloud and nursed his aching hand. On the bright side, she had not believed him when he'd revealed his feelings. Thinking he was no better than the rumors of his excesses, she would stay away from him and Ardmore Crest. Excellent. So be it. If he was careful, he might save himself and his future. From now on, he would give Milverly a wide berth. With any luck, Justine would be gone within a handful of weeks.

Justine thought of the stagecoaches stopping in Oldhaven every morning on the way to London. A quick, painless way to leave all the intolerable memories behind, she mused, but she could not abandon Nora. Not now when Henry had gone to Belgium on government business. Who knows when he would return?

Her eyes gritty from the lack of sleep, she stared out the window of her bedchamber at Milverly until dawn spread a faint light over the horizon.

Some people said dawn was the best time of day, a new beginning, a gift of another day, but to her it was painful. In the most vulnerable time of day, she could clearly see her shortcomings, her imperfections, and she wished she could dismiss the embarrassment of her feelings. Her love for an infamous rake could not strike pride in her chest, rather the opposite. Like a dog with its tail between its legs, she would have liked to slink away from Milverly and the village.

Out of the question, of course. She bided her time.

Two weeks passed, and she'd managed to stay out of Damien's way. Clara Trowbridge came for tea one day, but Justine took to her bed claiming a headache so that she didn't have to meet the old woman. Any reminder of Damien was to be avoided at all costs, she thought.

Lord Allenson came home earlier than expected, and

Eddie jumped up and down with excitement. Nora might have jumped, too, if it weren't for her unwieldy bulk. Justine felt a stab of envy at such devotion.

Henry, a stoutish man of middle height, curling brown hair, and warm brown eyes, enfolded his wife in a passionate embrace for all to see on the front step. Energetic, vociferous, and kind, he held a certain allure, Justine thought. No wonder Nora had fallen for the charming gentleman.

He bowed over Justine's hand. "Dear Sister, it is a great pleasure to have you here with us. Knowing you were here to aid Nora, brought peace to my mind. She's in good hands."

"It is wholly my delight, Henry," she said politely and meant it. She truly would have enjoyed herself if Damien had lived a thousand miles away, or at least fifty.

"Henry, you look tired and worn out," Nora said, leaning her belly against him. "Government business must lie heavily on your mind."

He did have the rumpled look of someone who had traveled a great distance. His coat, made from black superfine was creased, and his shirt points had lost their starch. "It was somewhat tedious, yes." He swung Eddie into the air until the boy squealed with excitement. "Dear boy, how you've grown!"

"Father, I'll soon be as tall as you."

Nora laughed and put her arm through Henry's. "Come, a hot meal, then rest."

Henry disengaged his arm. "Yes, sounds heavenly, my pet, but I've not come alone."

Justine noticed a slight gentleman standing by the coach in the gathering darkness. He wore an elegant brown coat and buff pantaloons. About five-and-twenty, Justine thought. His dark hair had been brushed forward in Brutus locks pomaded in place, and his thin face sported a long nose and wide lips. The eyes were gray and cautious, penetrating. A decisive gentleman of some power if his bearing was any indication.

"This is Mr. Garvey Shadwell, my new secretary. He

worked at the War Office before and left with glowing recommendations. I'm fortunate to have him on my staff at the Home Office. He's the youngest son of Lord Sweeney." Henry slapped the other man's shoulder and brought him to greet the family.

"I'm honored to meet you, Lady Allenson," Shadwell said smoothly and kissed Nora's hand.

"I know your sister, Mr. Shadwell. Elinor and I were presented the same year." Nora chattered about the spring of her coming out, and Shadwell smiled noncommittally.

He greeted Justine, an appraising look in his eyes. He nodded to her questions about the trip but was not very forthcoming, she thought. Evidently, Henry spoke enough for two men.

Eddie pulled the newcomer's arm and had to display a frog that lived an unhappy life in his pocket.

Henry laughed, and Mr. Shadwell smiled politely. He gave the deferential platitudes expected of an employee, and Justine deduced he had a talent for diplomacy.

Henry hoisted his son high on his shoulder, and the cavalcade advanced into the house.

"The crossing from Belgium was horrendous," Mr. Shadwell said to Nora's questions about their night on the packet. "We drew a sigh of relief when stepping onto British soil once more."

Justine noted that he had a tight voice, as if he often suffered pain or acute shyness. She joined in the conversation, and because of Henry's and Nora's gregariousness there was not a quiet moment at dinner.

Eddie had the great excitement of having his meal with the adults, a rare treat as he usually dined upstairs with his nurse. The somnolent air of Milverly received an infusion of life with the new arrivals.

"You will stay at home now, Henry?" Nora asked as Mr. Shadwell had excused himself after tea was served.

"Yes, my pet, I will work at home until the new infant has been born. That's why I brought Shadwell with me." He smiled proudly and patted his wife's large belly. His very un-British way of showing his emotions endeared him to

Justine. His Continental ways must stem from the many years he had spent abroad prior to his marriage.

Nora sighed. "I'm so relieved. Now I won't have to worry about you when the time comes. I have enough worries as it is."

The next morning, Justine overheard the gentlemen speak in the library as she approached on the terrace during her morning walk.

"The Fox will have to be found at all costs," Henry said forcefully. "The spy might be a danger to our hard-won peace; we know for certain that he's sending dispatches concerning our foreign affairs. Just as he once sold French government secrets to us, he's now keeping the Bonapartist fanatics informed of Jacobin sympathizers here. We will have to unveil the secret group."

"How do we know for sure that he's selling information, Lord Allenson?" Shadwell asked.

"A French informant in Castlereagh's pay has discovered the leak. He found out that the dispatches have been sent across the Channel from this area via a fishing vessel."

"That's why we came home early—that's why we're here," Shadwell said thoughtfully, "to learn the identity of the Fox."

"That's right. You'd better start asking questions of the locals. They would know if there's a stranger staying in the area or if something unusual is happening."

Justine stiffened, not wanting to reveal that she'd over-heard their conversation. They would be embarrassed, and so would she.

She hurried in the opposite direction. *A double spy? Living in these parts? Or did Henry only harbor suspicions that the spy worked on the Sussex coast?*

Her thoughts immediately went to Damien. He had acted in a very spylike manner that night when she'd had dinner at Ardmore Crest. The thought made her taut with worry. Then there was the valise . . .

Damien hated the very idea, but he had to ride over to Milverly and welcome home his best friend, Henry. There was no way he could excuse himself. Hoping that Justine would still be asleep, he rode over as early as he could without being rude.

He left his horse at the Milverly stables and entered through the terrace door as he heard Henry's cheerful voice coming from the library. The gloom that had shrouded his mind since his last argument with Justine lifted as he saw his friend and sensed the constant ebullience, the energy, in the plump body.

"Henry, you sly dog, sneaking home without as much as a note to announce your arrival. I heard from Struthers that you were back."

Henry's face lit up, and he flung his arms around Damien's shoulders. "You scoundrel!" he said. "Let me see if there are any new lines of dissipation on your face."

He studied Damien thoroughly, and Damien cringed, suspecting his friend would sense the heavy burden of his thoughts.

"No—you look in good health, but I hear you've stayed away from Milverly for weeks now. Nora is very put out with you."

"I've been busy with estate affairs, old fellow. Any new lines you see on my face are not from dissipation but from worries. . . ." He let the words peter out as he noticed the other man in the room.

"Shadwell, meet my oldest friend, Lord Lewington. We met when I was Eddie's age."

Damien nodded politely in greeting, feeling an instinctive dislike for the newcomer. A fox, he thought, always eager to nose into affairs that did not concern him. Shadwell gave a curt bow as if he returned the feeling of dislike.

"Shadwell is my new secretary. A real gem, if you must know, Damien. He keeps my government business in perfect order." He waved at the secretary. "Take a break, Shadwell. I'm sure you can find a mount to your liking in the stables. Great morning for a ride."

The secretary left.

"He rides?" Damien asked in surprise.

"He's a gentleman, not some backwater yokel. The

impoverished Lord Sweeney's youngest son. Had to take employment to stay afloat financially, but a gentleman, nevertheless. Worked at the War Office during the Peninsular War, then came to the Home Office, where I was fortunate to gain his services."

"Looks like a serious and close-mouthed fellow."

"It wouldn't do to employ a prattle-box in my line of work. He's a reliable man, very dedicated. Besides, Liverpool is an old crony of Sweeney. Bound to offer Sweeney's sons good positions."

Henry offered Damien a glass of port. "I'm delighted you came by this morning." He glanced toward the open terrace door and lowered his voice. "Nora thinks I'm here to await her confinement, which is true, but there's another reason. I've been told to flush out a spy that operates in these parts."

"Really?"

"The infamous Fox. Bonapartist sympathizers might try to bring Boney back from St. Helena, and that would not do—not do at all!"

"It's truly preposterous to think Boney has sympathizers in this country."

"True, nevertheless, Damien. There are Frenchies who are against the Bourbons, and overzealous Englishmen, Jacobin sympathizers—however much I loathe to make such an observation."

"Yes, hmmm, how true." Damien rubbed the back of his neck.

"You know everyone, Damien, and you have a good nose for crime. I would be grateful for your help. As a matter of fact, Castlereagh suggested that you be brought into the investigation. After all, you're used to intelligence work since the war."

He lowered his voice even further. "I need your help, old friend. There are rumors that a plot is hatched abroad to bring Boney back before the year is out. You know how dangerous that would be, and you don't know whom you can trust these days."

"You don't sincerely believe Boney could raise another army?" Damien asked, just to ask the question. He knew very well anything was possible regarding the volatile Frenchmen. He knew more than Henry would ever learn, but Damien could not speak of his own secret work for Wellington.

"I don't know," Henry said and rubbed his chin vigorously. "But I doubt it. The French army is denuded, exhausted, in low spirits. In all likelihood they would never march for Bonaparte again. But—"

"Of course, I will help you, Henry. I will do what I can."

Henry urged Damien to sit down in a chair by the fireplace and refilled his glass. "So, old fellow, what is new at Ardmore Crest?" Henry sat down in the opposite chair, his breeches straining over plump thighs.

The question was put in such a way that Damien suspected that Henry sought for more than just the latest gossip. "I think Ardmore Crest won't fall into the hands of the creditors after all. I've worked hard to improve the lot of the farmers, and the fields are producing more richly, thanks to new techniques. My debts will soon be paid, and my livestock expanded. Last year, I invested in the East India Company, and some shares have paid off handsomely."

"I always knew you would come about. You're a shrewd man, Damien." He leaned forward intently. "I heard rumors . . . romantic rumors that you squired my darling Justine around London for a time. I would be pleased to see her settled at Ardmore Crest, and I'm sure her father would have nothing against the match."

Damien stiffened, all the pain from his last meeting with Justine flooding back into his chest. "She . . . and I don't see eye to eye any longer. She is a diamond of the first water, a treasure for any gentleman who is fortunate to win her affection."

Henry narrowed his eyes, and Damien suspected he sensed more than the words had revealed.

"I think it's possible she has already given her affection to—someone." Henry's gaze grew sharper, more penetrating. "I don't know what ails her. She is a shadow of her former glorious self, and I must say I worry about her. I wish you could cheer her up."

Damien chortled. "You're about in your head, Henry. She'd rather see me dead!" He drank the rest of the port, savoring the feeling of warmth it spread in him, the softening it gave to his aching heart.

"Why?"

The simple question brought all his frustration to the surface, but Damien could not reveal the whole story to Henry. He was keeping secrets from his best friend, and he feared it might be the beginning to the end of their friendship, but he could not reveal all of his childhood fears that he'd carried with him into his adult life.

He heaved a deep sigh. "I'm sure you heard of my *acquaintance* with Justine in London. But you know me, Henry. I've always said I'll never get leg-shackled. I enjoy my life, my freedom. I never meant to court Justine; I only escorted her to a few balls and routs."

"Don't you want to settle down some day? A life of Cyprians, betting, and gambling is bound to jade the palate at some point. My life would be a wasteland without Nora and Eddie, and soon, the new infant."

Damien saw a way to drop the subject. "By the way, where is that little terror, Eddie, this morning? And my namesake, the worm?"

Henry chuckled. "He—closely attended by the worm—is driving his tutor to an early grave, I'll be bound." He stood. "But I won't let you leave before you've paid your respects to Nora. You have stayed away much too long. She'll never forgive you if you don't tell her the latest goings-on in the village."

"I'll leave that chore to Aunt Clara," Damien said dryly. "But I suppose I ought to do the pretty."

In a spurt of panic, regretting his visit to Milverly, he followed Henry. He should have waited for Henry to visit him at Ardmore Crest. *Don't lie to yourself, you coward. You could not stay away. Part of you is desperate for a glimpse of Justine*. Damien longed to silence that insistent voice, but he could only sigh in frustration.

Henry led him upstairs to the morning room where Nora usually met any visitors who happened to pass by before noon. He opened the door. "Look who I brought, Nora, darling."

Justine was there, sitting on the sofa next to Lady Allenson and holding up a tiny garment for inspection. Her face paled, and her lips turned downward at the corners.

He could barely stand to see the streak of pain in her glorious blue eyes. He had put that pain there, and it made him feel like a cad. Seeing her like that, holding that lacy nonsense in her hands, deepened his pain.

"Nora!" he said with mock cheerfulness. "You're certainly blossoming. I don't think I've ever seen you more attractive."

Nora swatted his hand as he held hers. "Don't lie to me, Damien! I'm as big as a sow, and no compliments will smooth over that fact."

"I do not make a habit of lying," he said and kissed her cheek. "There is a delightful bloom about your person, and soon you'll bring another scamp into this world to terrorize me."

Nora chortled. "Hmmm, one Eddie is enough. This will be a girl. I can feel it in my big toe."

Damien laughed and had to do the inevitable—take Justine's hand and pretend to kiss it. Say some polite phrases. Smile. He could get through it without a hitch.

He set a neutral smile on his face. "Miss Bryerly, you look as lovely as ever." At least that was true. "The country air has brought a gleam to your eyes."

"Unlike Nora, I'm not susceptible to flattery," she said coolly.

Nora tut-tutted. "All females are partial to compliments. Isn't that true, Henry?" She leaned against his side as he sat down next to her, draping his arm around her.

"I believe you're right, my pet. I found out early in life that compliments bring a speedy smile to the eyes of ladies."

"The born politician who knows exactly what to say," Damien drawled and sat down on the window seat, at an angle to Justine so that he didn't have to meet her gaze.

Justine's mouth worked as if she was struggling with her temper. "Flattery in itself is insincere. It is a device to gain favors from the recipient." She threw a dark glance at Damien, then averted her face.

Henry laughed. "Yes, and it works famously! Every time."

"Henry, you're incorrigible," Nora said, tweaking her husband's round chin. "But adorable nevertheless."

"Henry, I see that your absence has not dampened your wife's ardor," Damien said dryly.

"On the contrary! And my heart grows fonder every year. Nora is a true diamond. Always will be." He threw a shrewd glance at Damien. "I wish every gentleman to be as fortunate as I in choosing a wife."

Silence hung uneasily in the room, and Damien sensed that Justine was on the verge of exploding.

Justine could not stand the tension. She flung aside the infant's shirt and said, "I think it was not your flattery that won Nora over, Henry. You really meant everything you said to her. It is different when the flatterer only wants to gain his own end. Then, when he has achieved his goal, discard the object of his desire." She pinned Damien with a glare as she uttered the last words.

Henry sighed, his gaze traveling from Justine to Damien. "What you describe, Justine, is a rake, a libertine, someone without a heart."

She nodded, unable to say anything else lest she betray her emotions.

"Rakes are to be shunned at all costs, especially by virtuous maidens," Damien said, his voice cynical.

He stood abruptly. "Now that I've seen that you're in fine bloom, Nora, I will take my leave. You have only just reunited with Henry and must have a lot to discuss. I have business at home. An estate never rests."

"Bless you, Damien. I hope you won't continue to be a stranger here. I've missed you."

Damien did not respond, only bowed politely. He left without another glance at Justine.

Emotions churned in her chest, and she wondered if she would ever find rest from her inner turmoil.

"I'd say Damien has left a strong impression on you, dear Justine," Henry said.

"Well, you must be privy to the gossip." Justine glanced at Nora. "I have avoided the subject as you well know. Damien is the last person I want to discuss." With those words, she stood, not knowing how she could stand staying another hour in Sussex.

There was the matter with the valise—and the possibility that Damien was an infamous spy. She had a responsibility to divulge to Henry what she knew, and the longer she kept the valise a secret, the more difficult it was to step forward. If she did, would Damien be accused of treason?

Six

IN A DARK mood, Damien arrived home to find Roger in the library with a friend. The two young men were three sheets to the wind already, and an almost empty brandy bottle stood on the round marquetry table between them. The desk looked disheveled, as if the two men had searched for something.

Damien roared. "'Tis not even midday, and you are already well over the oar, Roger! It's totally beyond the pale. Get out, the both of you."

Roger rose unsteadily. "I live . . . here, too, big Brother. You can't . . . *hic* . . . throw us out. 'Twould be intolerably rude to our guest."

Damien strode to his side and gripped the front of Roger's coat. "I can and I will. For once you'll have to listen to me."

Roger steadied himself against Damien's shoulder. "You should at least do what is polite and greet my friend Graham Mount Hopper. Met him at . . . *hic* . . . Oxford. Hoppy, say hello to my irate brother, Lewington."

The other man, taller than Roger, and of athletic build, rose unsteadily. He gave a nod, and Damien could tell that he held his liquor better than Roger.

"Servant," Hoppy said, his voice slurring slightly, "dashed fine brandy you keep in these parts."

"I've told Hoppy all about the smugglers," Roger said with an inane smile.

"I'm sure you have," Damien said acidly and pushed Roger away from himself. His brother reeked of brandy, and Damien was disgusted with Roger's lack of control. He turned to the newcomer. "Have we met before?"

Hoppy shook his head. "I don't think so. I don't frequent London as much as I'd like." He put a slender hand on the back of a chair. Damien noted the cool expression in Hoppy's gaze as it landed on Roger. For a moment, Damien could not but wonder if they were friends or—enemies.

"I invited Hoppy to stay here for some time. He's courting a young woman in Brighton. Only a hop and a skip from here to Brighton. Hoppy . . . *hic* . . . hops . . . to Brighton." Roger laughed at what he thought was his clever turn of phrase, and Damien's fist itched to punch him.

Saves the fortunate Hoppy the expensive rent of Brighton lodgings for the summer, Damien thought. *A hanger-on?* He tried to gauge if the newcomer had chosen the good-natured Roger to pay his expenses for the summer, but the young man wore a coat of the finest cut, and there was no fault to be found with the rest of his appearance. No fault, except the cold eyes.

"Very well, but I won't have you drinking in the library before noon." He turned to the young Mr. Hopper. "Are you related to the Berkshire Hoppers?"

Mr. Hopper shook his head. "The family is from Oxfordshire. Father has"—he dragged out the word as if thinking hard—"owns property outside Faringdon."

He didn't say country seat, Damien thought, but that did not imply that Roger was sponsoring a mushroom. At least the young man seemed to have better manners than Roger; the friend bowed and led Roger outside through the terrace door. Damien made a mental note to have the hapless Hoppy investigated by a Bow Street Runner. While in his cups, Roger was liable to be taken in by every kind of trickster and fortune hunter.

This latest confrontation, on top of everything else, put Damien in a foul mood. He sat down at his desk feeling as if a thorn were festering under his skin, right above the heart.

The vitriol he'd exchanged with Justine Bryerly did not make his burden lighter. Guilt weighed heavily on him, and he wished he could find a way to make peace with her so that they both could get on with their lives. Unfortunately, life wasn't as simple, not when he was unsure of his feelings for her.

He had started to dislike her after their first confrontation at the inn, but also felt more drawn to her than ever, as if by getting to know her better, share her innermost feelings, he would end up knowing *himself* better.

He had to do something about it.

He might have to find the courage to court her again—if she would allow it. The thought left him cold with panic.

He slammed a knotted fist against the top of his desk so that the writing implements and candelabras rattled. He had to find a way to unclamp the vise around his heart, the legacy of his past. Damn it, he'd bruised his hand, *again!* He stared at the stack of papers littering the desk and wondered why Roger, or Hoppy, had riffled through them.

Nora and Henry spent most of the time in Nora's boudoir whispering and giggling like children. It made Justine feel old and ill-humored. Despite the current gloomy and rainy weather, she took to riding through the meadows toward the sea, and one morning she encountered one of her old friends, Charity Thornton, whose father owned a summer-house outside Brighton.

She viewed with delight the fair-haired lady wearing a blue riding habit and a hat with plumes dyed the same blue color. Charity's gray eyes twinkled with mirth.

"I didn't think you would have time to leave Nora's sickroom, Justine."

"Nora is doing very well, better than predicted, and now that Henry is back, she does not need me every hour of the day."

"I'm delighted. That means you can ride across to Jasmine Cottage soon and spend the day. So many of the fashionable people have taken lodgings in Brighton for the summer. Some of our friends visit me constantly. I wish it wouldn't rain so much."

"Yes, it rains every day. Henry says the crops will rot if the foul weather keeps up."

"Yes, but we can't let the weather stop our summer activities. Will you come for a picnic on the beach? If it starts raining, we'll move the picnic inside."

Justine brightened at the thought of getting away from Milverly for a day. "I will count the days."

Charity told her the date and time, then waved and rode off just as the heavens opened all the dams.

Nora expected the infant to be born any day now, but she urged Justine to take the opportunity to visit Charity and abandon her duties for one day. "It will do you good to see some old friends and forget your woes."

Justine stiffened. "I don't have any woes to speak of."

Nora tilted her head to one side and smiled. "I know you don't want to speak about it, but I understand that Damien hurt you deeply, and that he continues to do so. Mayhap it was a mistake to ask you to visit me."

Justine shook her head. "Not at all! I don't have to speak with him again. If he comes here, I shall plead a headache. Sooner or later, all will be forgotten."

Nora put her hand over Justine's. "You're so brave, but I know from experience that wounds of the heart heal slowly and—painfully."

Dangerously close to tears, Justine jerked her hand away. "I don't suffer from a wound! And I do not want to discuss Damien with you. He's your friend, and you'll defend him to your last breath."

"Damien is not the libertine he used to be. He has changed since he had to bring Ardmore Crest away from the brink of ruin."

"See? You're already doing it—defending him. Besides, I saw him kissing his mistress outside the inn at Fairhaven. In broad daylight. I don't think he has changed that much if he installs his mistress at the Fisherman's Luck."

"A gentleman has . . . er, needs. Most unwed men of

our acquaintance have mistresses, and most of them leave their paramours behind when they decide to marry and set up their nurseries."

Justine glanced at her sister suspiciously. "You do seem to know a lot."

"I am a married woman, and Henry has explained certain things to me about the gentlemen's world. Really, Justine, they are not all cold and selfish libertines."

Justine rose, for she could not longer stand her sister's scrutiny. "I am certain you're right," she said to end the discussion. "This conversation does not apply to my current situation, however. If you don't need me, I think I shall retire to my room." She pecked her sister dutifully on the cheek and fled.

If only Nora hadn't defended Damien, claimed that he'd turned over a new leaf . . . If only her heart didn't lurch every time she remembered him or thought she caught a glimpse of him in the village.

The next morning a benign fate brought sunshine and a capricious breeze, but heavy clouds loomed on the horizon. The oaks swayed in a graceful dance, and the shrubs dipped in curtsies as Justine walked to the stables to fetch Columbine, the sprightly mare. A groom would accompany her on her ride over to Jasmine Cottage.

She wore a pearl gray riding habit trimmed with blue braid. A beaver hat sat a rakish angle on her head, and the plumes perfectly matched the blue of the trim.

Feeling light at heart for once, Justine looked forward to seeing Charity again.

The cottage, which was truly a rather large elegant house, sat on top of a knoll by the sea. Outside the stone wall, a path wound through the gorse-covered dips and hillocks to the water. It ended by a beach, a flat stretch of black shale and glittering sea flanked by tall cliffs and boulders. *Privacy, and a perfect spot for a picnic on a sunny day,* Justine thought as Charity brought her party down the path. Footmen followed carrying hampers of food and drink.

Justine adjusted the collar of her riding jacket, wishing

she hadn't worn her habit. The sun beat down on the water, blinding her with its sharp glitter, but despite the slight discomforts, the morning had all the possibilities for enjoyment. She inhaled the sea scents with pleasure and watched others step along the path while talking in animated voices. The wind bore the words out over the cliffs.

Charity introduced Justine to the others as they arrived. "This is Roger Trowbridge and Graham Mount Hopper."

The two men bowed. "We've met," Roger said.

Roger still had Damien's grin, Justine thought with a stab of resentment. She forced herself to smile and greeted them affably. She would not let thoughts of Damien ruin her day.

"Call me Hoppy," Mr. Hopper said. "Everyone does." He gave her a charming smile that she somehow found rather calculated. His hand lingered a trifle too long on her fingertips. "You're staying at Milverly?"

"Yes, with my sister."

"I'm staying at Ardmore Crest, and I hope we'll find the opportunity to meet again—soon."

"I daresay I shall be rather busy," Justine replied dismissively. Hoppy looked handsome in a fine blue coat and a Belcher handkerchief tied around his neck. His hair had the artificial windblown look, and she noted that the real wind could not dislodge the careful arrangement. She did not trust gentlemen who spent much time in front of the mirror arranging their hair; nevertheless, she couldn't find fault with Hoppy's easy charm. He seemed much more worldly than his companion.

Roger Trowbridge stumbled for what at first seemed no reason; as he drew near, it was apparent that he bore a strong smell of wine on his breath. He gave her an inane smile. "I think we met at my aunt's dinner party. Am I right? What a rum gathering that was."

"Rum?" Justine asked.

Roger shrugged. "My aunt has a strange set of cronies, especially that puffed-up dragon, Lady Dunmore."

The lady in question stood with her "cronies" under a marquee that had been set up on a grassy strip right above the beach proper. "Your aunt is not here?"

Roger gave the group a hazy glance. "Don't think so, thank God . . . *hic*. His gaze roved to the hampers from which the footmen extracted wine bottles. "Would you like a glass of wine, Miss Bryerly?"

"Not yet, thank you." She gave Roger and his friend a smile and hurried away to greet the other guests, Lady Jamison and her daughter, Davina, and the Ladies Stansted, Dunmore, and Ludville, all stout women with piercing eyes and disapproving expressions. *Chaperoning their shy daughters,* Justine thought. The girls were old friends from the London season.

Two more gentlemen made up the party, local gentry that Justine had not met before, and Lady Dunmore's French companion, the mousy Monique. The flair and style of the French had completely passed by Monique, Justine thought, feeling sorry for the young woman whom Lady Dunmore no doubt bullied from morning till night.

"Monique de Vauban looks sad," she said to Charity.

"I would, too, if I had to live to fulfill Lady Dunmore's every wish. Monique had nothing but her clothes when she came here—a child rescued from the Terror. Every member of her family died except Monique. I try to cheer her up, but to no avail. She keeps very much to herself." Charity twirled her parasol and watched the silky fringe sway.

"She has no chance to meet eligible gentlemen. If she were married, she might be happier."

Charity's slim eyebrows rose in disdain. "Lady Dunmore would never accept losing her. Who would fetch and carry for no payment except board and castoffs?"

Monique must have sensed they were talking about her. She smiled sweetly, her dark eyes flashing for a moment before the eyelids came down to shield any further expression. She wore a rather outmoded gown of pale green sarcenet, an old bonnet on her tightly wound black hair, and a parasol with a frayed ruffled edge.

"If she cared about her appearance more, gentlemen would be drawn to her quiet beauty," Justine said right before they joined the group.

Charity only nodded her agreement.

"Miss Bryerly," Lady Dunmore said in her pompous voice, "how is Nora? I could send over Monique for a day to keep her company."

Monique gave another dimpled smile, and her dark eyes simmered with an emotion Justine could not read. Dislike? Worry? "Yes, I'm sure I could be of assistance to your sister in her time of need," she said tonelessly.

"*I'll* do the fetch and carry until the infant is born," Justine said with a pointed glance at Lady Dunmore. "But I would not mind knowing Monique better—if you care to spare her presence now and then, Lady Dunmore. She seems rather lonely."

"Hmph! I give her everything she needs. She's quite happy in my household, aren't you, Monique?" Lady Dunmore's protruding eyes challenged the younger woman who shrank back.

"Yes . . . very."

"Nevertheless, I would be pleased to have some company at Milverly. Please bring Monique when you visit next."

Lady Dunmore nodded curtly. "I shall see if we can find the time. Monique is a rather busy young lady."

Yes, mending linen and unpicking your untidy embroidery, Justine thought uncharitably. She could not abide selfishness, especially as it made a prisoner of a lady who surely longed for gaiety and entertainment.

Roger Trowbridge joined the group, interrupting.

"Miss Bryerly, let me assist you to the chair with the finest view of the sea," he whispered and took her elbow. She obeyed, but surely an opportunity would present itself to speak with the French lady again. Her tragic past intrigued Justine.

Smiling and chatting, Roger made himself useful by helping the older ladies into the chairs that the servants had brought down from the cottage. He knew how to charm, Justine thought, just like his brother.

"Isn't it a glorious day for my picnic?" Charity asked and patted the wide-brimmed straw hat on her head. It protected her from the strong sun. Justine adjusted the angle of her borrowed parasol to protect her complexion.

"It is. Charity, I didn't know you had made the acquaintance of Roger Trowbridge," Justine said. "When did you meet him?"

Charity laughed. "In Oldhaven. He has caught a fit passion for me, seldom leaves my side unless Father throws him out. He's rather adorable, harmless, in fact."

"Are you . . . well, interested in him?" Justine glanced at the high color on the young man's face and the hollow cheeks and feared that Charity might make a mistake settling her feelings on him.

Charity gave another laugh. "Hmm, I might find him attractive if he didn't look so deeply into the bottle. I've known him all my life. He's a friend, nothing more. I have told him so in no uncertain terms, but he still hangs at my side like a limpet."

"Very flattering to have such a devoted admirer."

"Roger's friend, Hoppy, is asking about you. Lady Stansted is telling him all the details of your great fortune, I'm sure. But I daresay he's bowled over by your dark beauty."

"Nonsense. Have you noticed he has the eyes of . . . of some cold predatory animal? Hoppy is not the type of gentleman who speaks to my heart."

Justine moved to the blanket tilting the parasol over her face. The breeze ruffled the fringe and brought the tangy odor of seaweed and salt to her nose. She inhaled deeply of the bracing air and felt her spirits lift.

"What kind of gentleman does?" Charity asked and sat down beside Justine. "A blond man; a short, fat man; or a young willowy sort?"

Justine chuckled, and thought about those descriptions. "Attraction is a difficult thing to define. Certainly it matters how the gentleman looks, but it's more the impression of the whole. Take my brother-in-law, Henry, for instance. Not exactly a handsome man, but so full of *life*."

She remembered Damien's charming smile, but she was not about to reveal her feelings about him to Charity. "I don't know. What do you think? I haven't met anyone lately who speaks to my heart."

"I remember how upset you were when Damien left London. Have you had time to get over him?"

Ah! Charity would bring it up, Justine thought, nodding quickly, too quickly. "I knew all along he wasn't worth my affection." She looked away to conceal her face from Charity's scrutiny. She took off her hat and unbuttoned her riding jacket. Underneath, she wore a white shirt with long sleeves, and she decided she would overheat in the sun if she didn't take off her jacket.

"When he smiles, my knees turn weak," Charity said with a sigh. "Why is it that we are drawn to gentlemen whose grins can make us swoon? How come a mere smile affects me in such a way?"

Justine shook her head in puzzlement. "I wish I had the answer to that! Are females really that weak? Don't we have any control over our hearts?"

Charity laughed. "You sound so glum, Justine. It isn't as dire as that. I don't fall in love with every wicked grin I see, and neither do you."

Justine joined in the laughter. "You're right! Your refreshing outlook on life raises my spirits." She glanced at her friend. "You said you were drawn to the marquess. Have you set your cap at him?"

"Oh, no! He has never looked twice in my direction. No, I have my eye on Jeremy Brandon in the next village." She made her voice dark and mock pompous as if mimicking her father. "He's a steady young gentleman of whom my parents would greatly approve. I daresay he would make a far better husband than a rake."

Justine nodded, her spirits plummeting once more. Their conversation ended as footmen brought around platters of food: cold pâté, roasted duck, boiled shrimp, bread, and cheeses that sweated in the heat. Justine accepted a glass of cold hock with which to wash down the food, and the wine went to her head rather too quickly.

"Miss Bryerly," Roger said, as the raspberry-flavored blancmange had ended the meal and the bowls had been removed, "how do you like these parts?" He sat down on the edge of the blanket and stared adoringly at Charity—

probably wishing he would dare to involve her in a discussion.

"It is lovely here. I never knew how beautiful Sussex was until my sister married and moved here. I also hear there is a great deal of adventure along the coast."

He flashed that wonderful Trowbridge smile. "I take it you're alluding to the smugglers. Yes, that is a trade that has gone on for centuries in these parts. Anything to avoid paying excise for tea and brandy, and other goods." He inched closer to Charity, who fluttered her eyelashes teasingly. No wonder the young Roger was smitten with the lovely Charity Thornton.

If Justine had hoped to gain more knowledge about the secret trade, she learned nothing more. If Roger or his elder brother were involved, he would not want to reveal any secrets. *Secrets!* The memory of the valise flashed through her mind. Someone would have to be informed . . . but who? The longer she put it off, the harder it got to reveal its existence.

She got up, leaving her spot to the hopeful Roger. "I shall take a stroll looking for shells." She went to the water's edge, and shielding her eyes with her hand, she tried to see if there were any hidden coves—smuggler's hiding places—among the cliffs.

Seagulls above and the restless sea below were the only things that moved. She picked up a handful of white and pink shells and walked past two tall boulders. Tawny sand had been pushed into rigid crests, echoes of the real waves, and she found more shells at the base of the cliffs.

Feeling slightly light-headed from the wine and the heat, she retraced her steps. She could hear the talk and the laughs. Glancing at the bobbing hats of the chaperones, she saw a tall figure standing behind them.

Justine's heart lurched as she recognized Damien. She touched her throat as if finding it difficult to breathe. The last person she wanted to see! Turning on her heel, she walked back to the concealing boulders. Charity had not mentioned that the marquess had been invited. Had the dratted friend planned to throw them together? Justine had no desire to speak with Damien in front of all these people.

She contemplated finding another path up the hill to Jasmine Cottage but realized there was only one way to reach the house from the beach. She heard the crunching of boots against the shale, and she knew who had sought her out.

A small smile played around Damien's mouth as he came around the boulder.

"Are you hiding from *me,* Justine?"

"Hardly," she said. "Don't think too highly of yourself. Not everyone is begging for your company. I would rather be alone, thank you."

She waited for him to obey her wish and leave, but he leaned his shoulder against the rough side of the rock. "I wish we could find a way to a truce. I have no desire to spar with you every time we meet, and we're bound to converge at times." He sighed as if frustrated. "I didn't know you were here; if I did, I would have stayed away. Honestly."

"I've made it my mission to avoid you, but I cannot control your movements in the area. And it is hardly my fault if we argue. Truth is, we cannot abide each other, and the natural course would be to stay away from each other."

"Another choice would be to behave in a civilized and polite manner."

"I have not struck you, have I? Nor have I shouted at you like a fishwife."

He heaved another deep sigh. "That's true, but I want us to be friends, just as I'm friends with Nora and Henry. Let's bury the past."

"If you think I worry about the past, you're sadly mistaken. I have other concerns, and you are not even dimly part of those concerns." She made as if to walk around him, but he stepped into her path, standing so close she could see the play of emotion—exasperation and longing?—in his eyes, and the broad chest heaving with his every breath.

"Your face is reddening from the sun," he said, a fingertip trailing the line of her jaw. She wondered if the chaperones could see them standing so close, but the boulder shielded them from view.

"I daresay I should fetch my parasol. I forgot it on the blanket," she said breathlessly as his gaze raked down the front of her white shirt. Her breasts tingled with anticipation, a novel feeling that worried her more than anything she'd ever experienced before. His gaze seemed drawn to her chest and stayed there, incensing her sensations further.

A flush rose in his cheeks, and his eyes darkened with passion. "You're lovely, Miss Bryerly. I have always thought so."

"I am not one of your lady 'friends'."

A smile pulled at his lips. "Have I ever suggested that you were?"

"No . . . but I imagine you would give no *lady* indecent glances." Was the squeaky voice really hers? She pushed him aside, but he caught her in his arms before she could round the cliff.

"Let go of me! What will the chaperones think of us? They will send someone to fetch us into full view."

"Not quite yet." He lowered his face to hers, his arms almost lifting her off the ground as he kissed her. Her head whirled as his tongue invaded her mouth in a most intimate manner . . . so rudely . . . so deliciously. Her knees buckled, and he held her up, crushing her breasts against him, kissing her face until she filled with an intoxication so sweet she thought she would surely melt.

She finally found the strength to break away from him as his hand curved around her breast and squeezed.

"Justine," he muttered, "you drive me insane with desire." His eyes held a dark and dangerous gleam, and she took one unsteady step back and spun around.

As tears choked her throat, she thought of running all the way back, but the chaperones would raise questions. She pretended as if nothing had happened and bent to pick up a shell from the water's edge. She had lost all the other ones during the kiss.

Charity waved, and she had to wave back, even though she longed to throttle her friend.

He fell into step beside her, sometimes bending to pick up a shell. She could feel the heat of his gaze and stubbornly kept her face averted.

Damien's heart thundered in his chest. He desired her as he'd never desired a woman before. Her innocence, coupled with the passion rising in her like fire, drove him wild. As he kissed her, he'd felt the need to discard all her clothes and make wild love in the sand, but that would never do. She would not take off her clothes for a man unless he was her husband. And she should not. She was a lady.

Yet he could not stay away from her. He'd tried, but she invaded his thoughts constantly. He would have to woo her again, find a way back to her frozen heart—and his—or go mad. The simple truth was, he could not live without her.

He had to retrieve what he'd lost by abandoning her in London.

Damien picked up a handful of shale and sifted it through his fingers. "I've never believed in love, Justine, or deep trust between two people. I don't know if I do now, but I want to."

She walked on, a stony expression on her face, her gaze fixed to the ground.

He'd never spoken to one of his women about his humiliating past, but he felt compelled to tell her. "My father was one like me, a rake who cared naught for the hearts of the ladies. He crushed my mother's heart, brought his light-skirts to Ardmore Crest—pardon my frankness—and showed Roger and me that a man could discard women as often as he discards his soiled linen."

"So you had to do the same?" she asked, her voice less scathing than it had been earlier.

"A boy looks to his father for guidance. It is natural. I drank and I gambled, just like my father. Roger is doing the same. I am known for my many mistresses, and when I tire of one, I easily find another. Just like Father." It pained him to talk about the past, of the rotten core of his family. It hurt to admit to weakness, but he had to explain everything to her so that she believed him. "I have changed, I'm no longer—"

"Your father died rather young," she interrupted. "Is that your goal as well?"

Damien shook his head, determined not to let the discussion bring on one of his black moods or his temper. "No . . . I have curbed my drinking to a minimum, and I cannot afford to gamble any longer."

"But you keep a mistress." She gave him a challenging stare. "Don't deny it. I saw you in the village."

"You're right," he said with a sigh.

"So you haven't changed, not really. Don't try to pull the wool over my eyes."

"I *have* changed! I care more about the future of Ardmore Crest and all the people who are dependent on me than I do about pleasuring myself." He wished he could show just how much he'd changed, but he read only skepticism in her eyes. "And I care about you—deeply."

Justine wished she could believe him, but doubt lodged in her heart. "I can't believe everything you say. Action speaks louder than words. Besides, why should I care? I don't understand what part I play in this new vein of 'confession.' You are revealing rather sordid truths, unfit for a lady's ears."

He stopped, and she had to halt, too, as she was curious to hear his answer. He turned toward the sea, looking out over the restless, glittering water. The waves frothed and rustled at their feet.

"You're right, but it is important. Mayhap I want you to really know me, not just the character I play in the great theater of society. Father taught me that *love* did not exist, only lust. Use the women and discard them. I believed him. I've never loved, but now I think something is happening to my cold heart." He glanced at her with narrowed eyes, and Justine fought an urge to cry. "It started happening in London with you, and I panicked, not knowing where to turn with my softening heart."

Tears burned behind her eyes.

He continued, "I don't know what it is, and the strong emotions are making me afraid."

"Afraid of what?" she asked as a need to touch him came over her. She did not touch him, rather took a step away from him.

"Afraid of where they might lead. Will I become a slave to my emotions, lose control of my life, a control gained with such difficulty?"

He bared his very soul to her in that moment, and she watched the stark expression on his face as a wave of compassion washed through her.

"I don't know," she whispered. "But if the love is shared by two people, won't it carry, hold them both—forever?"

He pushed his hand through his wind-whipped black curls. "I would like to find out."

"Perhaps you will, but I want no part of your life at this point. I cannot really believe you've changed until I see evidence of your new ways. For all I know, you might make up a story to ignite my compassion. Rakes are experts at worming their way into a woman's heart. Not only that, but you might not be who you say you are—a lawful citizen."

She almost blurted out the secret of the valise but kept silent at the last moment.

He chuckled dryly. "Lawful citizen? I daresay you're hinting at the smuggling activities in the village. Don't worry, I won't do anything foolhardy that will bring the hangman's noose around my neck."

He might be lying. He was *lying,* she thought. She had proof in that valise. The hope that had risen with his baring of his soul, evaporated. She could not trust this handsome, passionate, utterly charming man, no matter how much her heart yearned for his embrace.

The thought depressed her no end, and she wished she could throw caution the winds and believe him. But if she did, would he burn her once again?

Seven

IN HER DREAMS, Justine relived Damien's stricken expression on the beach as she'd denied him her trust—and her love. She tossed and turned, unable to find the peace she sought. Had she made a mistake? That suspicion gnawed on her consciousness, but what was done was done? She had made a choice not to let him into her heart, and now she could not change her mind. She might be temperamental, but never fickle.

With a sigh, she swung her legs over the side of the four-poster bed. If she was to get any sleep at all tonight, she'd better heat some milk. She could have called for Agnes to accomplish the chore, but she didn't want to speak with anyone. She swept a wrapping gown around herself.

Carrying a lit candle, she went downstairs. The kitchen smelled of onion, and the heady aroma of newly baked bread lingered under the rafters. A banked fire still glowed in the hearth, showing her the way across the room.

She found an ewer of milk in the larder, a plate covering the top. She poured some in an iron pot and set it to heat by the fire. Spying half a raspberry pie in a dish on the table, she cut herself a large wedge. Her mouth watered at the thought of the clandestine treat. She would act irreverently uncouth and eat it with her fingers.

The night had the oppressive air of an approaching thunderstorm. Looking through the window, she saw no stars, no moon. The clouds smothered the sky outside, and nothing stirred. She cautiously opened the back door and stepped out. This door faced the stable yard and the enclosed herb garden, of which one corner wall had been cemented to the house itself.

A green wooden door led into the garden, and on impulse, Justine stepped along the brick path and through the door opening. From past experience, she knew the herb garden gave out an intoxicating aroma, and she enjoyed it now. She walked among the rosemary bushes and hardy thyme, tender basil, and spicy marjoram.

Despite the oppressive air, Justine delighted in the feeling of freedom. No one was present to berate her for her lack of decorum. The house at times seemed to shrink, the walls to hem her in until she could not breathe. Fanciful thoughts mayhap, but she relished this small respite from duty and etiquette.

The milk must be warm enough to drink now, she thought, and headed back toward the door.

A shadow flitted on the wall by the door, and she almost screamed in fright. Clamping her hand to her throat, she stared aghast as a tall figure, that of a man wearing a cloak, moved swiftly toward her.

On the secluded beach below the Crest, Damien stared out to sea and kept an eye on the fishermen's work. The waves frothed and roiled against the shore as the smugglers unloaded the rowboats that went out to the French lugger and returned with bales of silk. Damien had received the information that the French wanted to strike a deal over the extra silk, even though it was not the usual time for a delivery. It would be much needed additional income for the smugglers.

He had to rendezvous with the Frenchman who, against generous payment, regularly provided the Foreign Office with information about Bonaparte's life on St. Helena. Jacques would be on the lugger with his latest information.

He also carried bulletins to Wellington in Cambrai, bulletins that Damien collected in Crawley from various sources. Damien had known Jacques many years, his most valuable contact during the war. Jacques was not the Fox. Damien was sure the Fox carried a British name.

Damien addressed the French captain who came in with the second trip to settle the deal. "Is Jacques with you tonight?"

The captain snorted. "Ze man is always complaining! Small waves, big waves, *le diable* always suffers *mal de mer*." He shrugged. "But he's on ze boat, waiting to meet you, Monsieur."

A cold shiver traveled up Damien's spine. How would he explain the loss of the coded reply to the last French dispatch? Without the reply, the spy did not know what his next assignment would be. *Damn Roger,* Damien thought then cursed himself for sending his younger brother. to Crawley to pick up the payment for the last shipment, which also included the message.

Communications went through the wholesale merchant in Crawley, and Damien had never met any of the men working at the other end, the secret connections to the government—spies like himself. He rather liked the word *patriot*. They worked for the good of Britain.

And now the Fox was selling information about British foreign policy to the French. The man would have to be found or the spy network set up with such difficulty in Paris might be penetrated—if it wasn't already—and the spies' lives endangered.

Worried, Damien inhaled the tangy sea odors and waited until the last bales had been unloaded. He paid the Frenchman for the haul and went into the rowboat to meet with Jacques on the lugger.

The French spy had a long thin nose in a narrow face, quick brown eyes, and an agile body. He looked pale and haggard in the light from the lantern. A knit cap covered his curly hair.

"*Bonsoir, monsieur.*" He took a packet of papers from a leather satchel and handed them silently to Damien.

"Thank you, Jacques. I don't have any further instructions this time. An unfortunate delay at the other end. Take a rest and meet me again at the dark of the moon." He placed a heavy purse in the Frenchman's hand. "I take it Boney is still on St. Helena? Not hatching more plans for escaping?"

Jacques showed a row of white teeth. His eyes flashed. "I will kill heem!" He stabbed his thumb into his chest. "*Moi*. If he returns to France! He murdered *mon frères,* and Jacques never forgets. *Jamais.*"

Damien felt the other man's desperation and pain and knew how many lives that madman Napoleon had destroyed. Families on both sides of the Channel had been torn apart, never to unite again. Losses too horrendous to even contemplate. He pumped Jacques's hand, wishing he could say something that would soothe the pain in the other man's eyes. *I have to find that valise, or Jacques's life might be in jeopardy. He could already be a marked man if the valise has been found by the enemy. The Englishman who sold his own country's secrets to the enemy . . .*

Rage filled Damien at the thought. "Jacques, be careful. There's a spy, a British spy, who is undermining the network. They call him the Fox, *le renard.* Have you any knowledge of him?"

Jacques's face tightened as he heard of the traitor. "*No.* I shall seek answers in Paris."

"As I said, be careful. I'll see you again in two weeks."

Jacques jingled his purse, generous payment for his dangerous work. "I'll return, be sure of that. *Au revoir.*"

Damien thanked the captain and left, the rowboat only a deeper shadow on the shadowy sea. As he reached the shore, big warm raindrops started falling. Thunder tore through the sullen sky, a sound like sailcloth ripping. A flash of lightning lit up the night, and he noticed flashes of lanterns farther down the beach.

"Get on with it," Damien said to Ben Bryman, the leader. "Push the pony train inland immediately. Hide the bales in the abandoned granary on my property and disperse. The excisemen have sniffed out our whereabouts."

Without another word, the smugglers hurried off in the

dark, pulling their sturdy ponies along, one tied to the other with silk bolts wrapped in tarpaulins strapped to their backs. The ponies wore rags tied around their hooves to silence the hoofbeats.

Damien climbed onto his horse and rode up into the hills bordering the sea. He stopped on a knoll and looked back. There was no sign of the smugglers, and the excisemen advanced on foot too slowly to catch up with the gentlemen.

The excise militia evidently had not understood—yet— that they had almost stumbled upon the pony train. They patrolled the beach at all times, and kept an outlook for strange vessels along the coast. The French luggers doused their lights as they came close to shore. Navigating in the dark was dangerous on an overcast night like this. Underwater reefs riddled the shoreline, and the currents could pull the boats to their destruction.

A dangerous way to fill one's purse, Damien thought, but he did not regret his involvement. Part of his work involved keeping England safe from such a man as Napoleon Bonaparte. He made sure the packet of foreign correspondence rested snugly in his cloak pocket.

He would not let it out of his sight until it could be delivered in Crawley. *Who knows where the traitor would turn up to snoop around? He would reveal himself sooner or later, and that would be the end.* Damien swore he would discover the identity of the man who sold information about his country to the enemy.

Justine stared in fear at the advancing man dressed in black. Her heart raced, and her mouth turned as dry as sawdust.

"Who goes there?" a male voice asked suspiciously.

Justine's knees tried to buckle under her, but she held herself up by leaning against the wall. Relief washed through her as she recognized Mr. Shadwell's voice.

"Oh, it's you," she said, her hands trembling. "You frightened me."

"What are you doing outside in the middle of the night, Miss Bryerly?" he asked harshly.

"Taking a breath of fresh air. I couldn't sleep. No crime in that, surely."

"No, I suppose not. But you never know who might lurk outside at night."

Justine remembered her state of undress and hurried past Henry's secretary as soon as her legs took on their normal solidity. "Then what are you doing out so late?"

"I suffer from insomnia and, like you, needed some fresh air," he said with a sigh and followed her through the door in the garden wall.

She thought he looked as though he'd traveled a long distance with his air of dishevelment, but she didn't say anything to the effect. Reluctant to give him a closer look at her dishabille, she halted outside the kitchen door in the shadows. He hesitated on the steps.

"I'll go around to the side door," he offered, evidently sensing her discomfort.

"Good night," she said. She stared after him; she knew that he'd not just left the house for a leisurely walk. He'd been gone for some time. In the weak light coming from the kitchen window, she'd seen the spatters of mud on his cloak and on his face. Mr. Shadwell, the taciturn secretary, whom she knew so little about harbored a secret, be it innocent or traitorous. Was there more to this man than met the eye? He seemed highly reluctant to reveal anything about his past, but she'd thought it stemmed from his station as Henry's servant.

Feeling weak after the fright, Justine sighed deeply. She stumbled inside and locked the door. She found a mug for the milk. Carrying her drink and a plate of pie, she hurried to her room.

At about the same time, Damien stepped into his library, still wearing his cloak. In the chairs by the fireplace slept Roger and his young friend, Hoppy. *The man of the ridiculous nickname,* Damien thought with a silent snort.

He debated waking them, but decided against it. He did not have the stomach to hear inane drunken speech so early in the morning, especially when he was as sober as a judge.

He viewed the two men and counted the claret bottles on the floor. Eight. *Four-bottle men,* he thought, not amused. *They are bound to feel liverish in the morning.*

He turned to leave, then noticed the mud on Hoppy's Hessian boots. The greenhead wore his clothes with style, and the muddy boots gave a jarring note to his appearance. Not only that, the mud had not yet dried. Where had the young man been in the last hour? Spying on the beach?

Damien changed his mind about letting peace reign. He gripped Hoppy's shoulder and shook him vigorously. Hoppy's eyelashes fluttered artfully as if he struggled with deep sleep.

Roger moaned in the chair beside Hoppy's. Damien gave him a hard shake as well. "Wake up you cod's heads! No need to spend the night in chairs like old men who can't walk up to their beds."

Roger opened one eye. "What's the matter with you, Dam? Don't shout! My head will crack open."

"I will crack it for you if you don't get going."

Hoppy stretched his arms over his head and yawned. "What time is it, Lewington?"

"You, if anyone, should know that," he said scathingly. "I can tell you haven't slept here all night."

"Where would I have slept? I didn't go out," Hoppy said, making round eyes.

"I beg to differ. My housekeeper does not leave a puddle of mud on the floor, so you must have ruined your boots elsewhere. What I want to know is, *where?*"

Hoppy gave him a look full of calculation and anger. "I don't think I have to report my whereabouts to you, Lewington." He struggled to his feet, his face reddening with anger.

"As long as you stay in my house, I feel a certain responsibility for you. I would like to know what kind of mischief goes on around here. If you're Roger's bosom bow, I know you're involved in all kinds of pranks."

"Zounds, Damien, don't rip into him like that! We went down to the village and comported ourselves with utmost decorum at the tavern. Ask the proprietor if you don't believe us."

Damien glanced from one innocent face to the other, knowing that slyness lurked behind the innocuous facades. "Yes . . . I might very well verify this with Mr. Birtle tomorrow." He pinned Hoppy with a hard stare. "If I discover that one of the maids of the estate is in the family way when you leave——" He let the word hang, wishing suddenly that the man *would* take himself off.

Hoppy did not inspire a reform of Roger's behavior, rather the opposite. They were leading each other to the shadows of hell where the bottle became the master and the man lost himself. It pained him to see Roger's pale, haunted face, as if the destruction was already nipping at his heels.

"You can't treat Hoppy like that, Dam! He's *my* guest, and I resent your hints that he should remove himself from the premises. And we haven't mauled any maids."

Damien realized that evicting Hoppy would mean Roger would leave Ardmore Crest as well. Under the circumstances, Damien preferred keeping an eye on his brother. He hoped to see the end of Roger's descent into the abyss of debauchery. He'd do just about anything to stop it.

"Very well, I might have spoken too harshly. I do not like to find you in my library imbibing wine at all hours of the night. Please remove the empty bottles before Struthers comes in here in the morning. I cannot abide the ensuing gossip, you see."

Roger grumbled something and nudged Hoppy with his elbow. Together the two men bent to retrieve the empty bottles. Damien hoped the small exertion would bring on a severe headache. Roger did look pale as he straightened his back. A slightly green tint colored the skin around his mouth.

"You'd better go upstairs and sleep off the effects of the wine."

As they left, Damien noticed that Roger's boots were muddy as well.

Damien sat down at his desk as the young men closed the door. He hauled the packet from his pocket and studied the sturdy brown wrapping paper. An urge to read the coded letters came over him, but he suppressed it. His part was not to decode the messages, only deliver them safely to the merchant in Crawley. He'd make sure that they landed in the right hands and that any new messages for Jacques would come to him personally. However much he resented showing that he'd failed, he had to add a note to the foreign secretary that the last coded message had gone missing.

Eight

THE NEXT MORNING, Nora said to Justine, "Now that Henry is here to support me, I think it would be a good idea for you to take Eddie to Grandmother Allenson at Haywards Heath. It would be a change of scenery for you, and Eddie would be delighted to see his grandmother."

Justine looked closely at her sister who was propped against the pillows in her enormous shell-shaped bed. Nora had a drawn look about her mouth, and her skin lay like a pale mask on her face.

"Has your time come?" Justine's heartbeat accelerated with anxiety.

Nora nodded. "I think so. The pains come and go. Henry has sent for the doctor and the midwife." She bit her bottom lip as she pulled up her knees to meet her large belly. "I would prefer it if Eddie left for a few days. Until this is over."

"Yes, of course . . . but I thought you needed me here, Nora."

"I did, but now that Henry is home, he shall look after me. I can't burden you with the responsibility of the household."

"I wouldn't mind. Managing the household would not be a burden." Justine noted the small frown on her sister's perspiring brow. "But I will comply with your wish, Nora.

I want you to feel safe and not have to worry about Eddie during a difficult time like this. I shall take him to Enderby."

Justine had placed her right hand on the coverlet, and Nora patted it. "I knew I could count on you. No woman could ever have a better sister." She leaned back against the pillows. There was a commotion on the stairs outside.

"There they are now. Henry has asked Shadwell to accompany you and Eddie on the trip, along with Eddie's nurse, Mattie, and your own maid. Grooms will ride along to protect you if need be. Shadwell will stay at Enderby until we send word he's to escort you and Eddie back here."

"I shall pray for you that everything goes well." Justine kissed Nora's perspiring brow as the door opened and the doctor entered. Henry strode in close on his heels, gesticulating. He was red in the face with worry.

He turned to Justine as she stepped toward the door. "Shadwell knows what to do. Everything has been prepared for the trip." He embraced Justine hastily and kissed her cheek. "Don't worry. Nora shall get through this ordeal. 'Twill be easier this time than when Eddie was born."

Justine smiled. "Take your own advice, Henry. Do not worry."

Some time later, under the sharp eye of the morning sun, the equipage set off. Shadwell and one groom rode beside the carriage. While Justine's thoughts lingered with her sister, Eddie prattled without stopping.

"I hope George, the footman, remembers to give my toads water while we're gone. I asked him to catch some flies as well, but he only laughed." Eddie's eyebrows pulled together in a frown. "He should be whipped for insubordination."

"Eddie!" Justine admonished. "Where have you learned such expressions? We don't whip our servants." She exchanged an amused glance with Mattie, the nurse.

"Shadwell said it to Papa."

"Well, you shouldn't listen to your father's conversations with Shadwell. They are not meant for your ears." Justine glanced out the window to make sure the taciturn secretary was out of earshot. "Very rag-mannered to eavesdrop, you know."

"Shadwell does not like my toads."

"He's a sensible man. Only small boys like toads for pets."

Eddie pouted. "That's not true! When I grow up, I will have a whole family of toads—"

"Living where?" Justine interrupted, unable to hold back her mirth.

Eddie scowled. "You're laughing at me! I will build a pond for the toads and catch flies for them."

"You will be hard at work then, from morning 'til night." Justine lowered her teasing voice. "A worthy purpose in life—toad farmer."

Eddie was at the point of giving her a fierce grimace, but he sighed and pulled at his starched shirt under the diminutive jacket of green velvet. "How long until we get to Grandmother Allenson's? It's so hot."

The sun was unusually piercing, and a heavy humid air had settled over the area. Not a leaf stirred in the still air.

"We'll be drenched before long," Agnes said wisely and peered at the hazy blue sky. "There's thunder in the air. My bones always ache before a storm."

"No . . . you must be mistaken," Justine said, but the air pressed around her like a blanket, and her skin under the thin muslin gown and silk pelisse grew clammy. She untied her bonnet of matching blue silk and took it off. The maid gave her a disapproving frown, but Justine ignored her.

"It's but a short trip. We shall reach Enderby before the storm has time to gather on the horizon."

"We shall see," Agnes said sagely.

"Do the smugglers go out in rainstorms?" Eddie asked.

Justine shook her head. "I doubt that, but I know very little about the smugglers' habits."

"I heard Papa say the smugglers were out last night. The troop of excisemen almost caught them red-handed."

"Were you listening at keyholes, Eddie?"

"No, he spoke with Shadwell before we left. He sent a

valise full of papers with Shadwell, telling him to get everything copied for the ministry."

"Shadwell does important work for your father, and for the country," Justine explained. "He is a very clever gentleman."

"I don't like him," Eddie said with a pout.

"Why is that?"

"He always looks at me as if I have done something I ought not do." Eddie's lips trembled. "I will never become a secretary. I shall become a hunter and a sportsman or a sea captain. Then there will be plenty of water for my toads."

"I see. Well, yes, I declare that sounds adventurous enough. You shall sail me and the toads to the Mediterranean Sea one day."

"*You,* Auntie Justine?" He made a face of disgust. "I won't allow girls on my ship."

Justine thought of a clever reply, but Nurse Mattie quieted her charge, and Eddie settled in his corner playing with a wooden soldier wearing a dragoon's uniform.

Justine dozed in the opposite corner as the coach made quick progress along the road. The heat grew more oppressing, and within the hour, heavy pewter clouds had risen on the horizon. Before long, the morning, which had been so bright, fell into a twilight gloom, the air sticky with humidity.

Worried, Justine glanced out the window. "We won't get there before the storm," she said to no one in particular.

"Just as I predicted," Agnes said with a small sniff.

"We should find cover." Just as she said that, the first lightning bolt embroidered the sky with silver. Thunder followed quickly, a deep rolling sound that echoed in the valley.

Shadwell rode up to the window. "We ought to take shelter somewhere."

"He should have thought of that earlier," Agnes said dourly. "Won't be a minute now before the deluge."

Justine had a censoring word on her tongue, but as rain started falling, she said nothing.

"There's an inn half a mile up the road. We shall stop

there until the roads are dry again. This storm will abate soon!" Shadwell shouted over the rapidly increasing downpour.

The coachmen slowed the horses to a walk, but Justine noted the wheels jolting through the potholes, and sometimes the coach seemed to lose its contact with the ground. *Mud,* she thought. *The road is turning into mud.*

She had barely finished the thought as the carriage careened sideways and came to an abrupt halt. Fortunately, the horses stopped immediately before the traveling chaise could be pulled over onto its side. An ominous creaking sound came through the window.

Justine jostled against Agnes's sturdy frame, and Eddie slid to the floor as he was lighter than the rest of the passengers. The vehicle remained in a slightly tilted position.

Shadwell opened the door. The rain had drenched him. His cloak hung in soggy folds, and water dripped from the rim of his hat. "Are you hurt?"

"No," Justine shouted over the drumming of the rain on the coach. "What happened?"

"It looks like one of the wheels broke as the coach went through a hole, Miss Bryerly. I shall take you and your ladies to the inn on my horse, one at a time."

Justine stared at Shadwell's dark eyes under the rim of the dripping beaver hat. He returned her gaze solemnly. She did not know why, but she shivered with apprehension. This journey seemed doomed before it had barely started.

"Very well, we might as well get on with it. Best start with Nurse Mattie and Edward. We don't want him to catch a cold. The sooner he gets out of the rain, the better."

Justine helped the nurse to sweep Eddie into a cloak. "Look upon it as a grand adventure," she said and pushed the boy's hat low over Eddie's ears. "There! Be good now and obey Mattie's every command."

"Must I?" Eddie asked with disgust in his voice.

Justine's reply drowned in the rolling thunder. Eddie's eyes widened with fear as lightning blinded the occupants of the coach.

Mattie carried him outside and ran through the rain to the horse. Shadwell lifted them up and set off along the road at a brisk pace.

"Mayhap it would have been better to wait out the storm here," Justine said to her maid. The coachman and the groom looked dripping wet as they tried to lift the carriage out of the hole.

"We don't know how long the storm will last. It might be over in a minute or it might keep raining until tomorrow."

Justine stared at the swaying gray curtain of rain and wished she'd known about the change of weather. She noticed a movement at the curve in the lane, a lone rider coming up behind them.

The powerful horse galloped through the puddles, but the rider pulled in the reins as he came upon the stranded carriage. He pushed his hat back from his forehead, and Justine stared straight into Damien's wet face.

"Damien! What are you doing out in the rain?"

"I could ask the same of you, but that would be prying," he drawled, immediately setting up her hackles.

A pain akin to longing constricted her chest, and she found it hard to breathe under his hard gaze. So much had been unspoken between them, so many emotions unresolved, that she felt the burden almost like a physical entity on her shoulders.

He scanned the area and got down from his horse. Water dripped in rivulets down his body and that of the mount. "Are you alone with the servants?"

She nodded. "Yes, but Shadwell took Eddie to the inn up the road. He'll be back shortly to—"

"I shall take you to him now." He opened the door, and rain sluiced through the opening.

"I will be drenched. I did not bring a heavy cloak since the trip should have been completed shortly."

"You can wear mine." He proceeded to undo the tie at the neck and swept off the cloak. His coat underneath was already wet on the shoulders, and it wouldn't be long before he was soaked through.

"I can't—" she started.

"Don't argue," he barked as if tired of her protests. "Come along." He gave her blue silk bonnet to her, swung the heavy cloak around her, and lifted her from the coach. "I'll be back for you in a minute," he said to the maid.

Justine felt his hard grip on her waist and missed his touch when he released her. As she fastened the strings of her bonnet, he wrapped the cloak tightly around her neck and tied it closed. It was wet, but still a temporary protection against the downpour. Rain drummed against her bonnet.

His cool fingers brushed her face, and she looked into his shadowy eyes, reading the concern, but also the strain, as if her presence brought nothing but frustration to his life. His cloak smelled of him, of soap, and of horse.

She did not protest as he lifted her onto his mount. Rain pelted her mercilessly. The wide hat brim shielded her face, but the water ran in small rivers down her neck. *Cold and unpleasant,* she thought.

He sat behind her, holding her tightly against him. The saddle chafed against her leg as she sat sideways leaning against him, but there was no need to complain during the short trip.

"What made you drive out in the rain, Justine?"

"Nora is confined, and she asked me to take Eddie to Enderby. I'm sure we will soon have word that Eddie has a new brother or sister." She clasped her hands together tightly. The strength of his arms around her, and her back against his strong chest, gave her great comfort.

"You're tense," he said.

"Wouldn't you be? Childbearing is fraught with danger. I would not want anything to happen to my sister."

He squeezed his elbows against her sides as he maneuvered the horse along the muddy road. "Don't worry. Nora is strong. She'll be up and back to normal presently—with another little terror at her apron strings."

Justine could not stop herself from laughing. "I'm sure you're right, but I cannot help but worry about her."

His voice came close to her ear. "It gives you credit to show such a degree of compassion. Do you feel any compassion for me?"

She did, but also great apprehension. There were their unsolved emotions, but also the question of whether he was involved in traitorous activities. "Why should I?" she asked cautiously.

"That I had to interrupt my journey to rescue you."

"Not compassion. Guilt is more like it," she said. "If I had known it would rain, I would have postponed the trip to Enderby."

"Think about it. I will have to face Eddie and his pranks."

Justine could not help but laugh, then tasted the rain. "Yes, he can be quite a trial. I daresay he released your namesake in the garden yesterday."

Damien laughed. "The worm?"

"Yes." She brushed away the wetness from her face. "He's now collecting toads. Very likely two of them have our names."

"Are those two a couple?" His voice was no more than an insinuating whisper against her ear, barely cutting through the drumming of the rain on the leaves.

She stiffened as a delicious shiver traveled through her body. "Hardly likely. They were chosen at random and now reside in a box by the pond."

"You don't think they will take to each other?"

"Mostly likely they'll end up fighting viciously."

"Your view is rather depressing, Justine."

"I'm only stating the most probable outcome. You cannot hold that against me."

"No . . ."—she sensed him shaking his head as he spoke—"but I had hoped for a more romantic view perhaps. I have always known you to be a soul full of passion and one who loves adventure."

He was right. Sometimes her feelings took her too high and to such giddiness that she knew she would fall. She had in the past. "I used to be someone who reveled in dares and adventures, but pain has tempered me, made me cautious. A totally new sentiment. I am not the same reckless person you knew in London."

"You have acquired a stillness that you did not have before. Call it a restful side that I find highly attractive."

She could not think of anything to say. That stillness had been hard won, and now he was about to threaten it. Every time he was near, her serenity was in danger of shattering. As it was right now. She would not become dependent on his feelings—or lack of them—again.

"I spent these weeks at Milverly trying to evade you—" she began, but he interrupted.

"And fate finds ways to continuously throw us together. Mayhap we should reexamine the reasons. Mayhap fate is of the opinion that we belong together?"

"I don't believe that for a moment." Justine closed her eyes. *No, I don't believe!* she repeated to herself. *Don't be fooled by your heart again. Don't give in.* She opened her eyes and saw a building surrounded by trees, a half-timbered house with a steep thatched roof. "I think I see the inn."

He did not say anything else, only turned the horse through the gates to the courtyard. He lifted her down by the door, and she rushed into the shelter. The taproom smelled of ale and smoke. Eddie sat by the fireplace, a blanket wrapped around him. The rain had glued his brown ringlets to his brow.

"Auntie Justine! Shadwell let me hold the reins of his big horse all the way."

Justine smiled ruefully. "I'm glad you didn't get lost on the way."

"The big brute obeyed me at every turn," Eddie said gleefully.

Justine laughed and shook out the wet cloak. "You sound just like your father. Big brute, indeed. I think Shadwell has a handsome horse." She turned to the secretary. "Thank you for taking such good care of him. Lord Lewington happened to come along and help me."

"I'll fetch the luggage. We'll have to stay here until I've rented another equipage, Miss Bryerly. And I shall speak with the local wheelwright."

She glanced over her shoulder for Damien and noticed that he'd already gone back. His cloak! He'd forgotten his cloak or felt that she needed it more. The thought warmed her heart. She patted the garment and hung it over the back of a chair to dry.

The landlord brought warm milk for Eddie and a wedge of currant pie. Justine ordered tea and more pie. The ordeal had made her famished. She brushed back damp tendrils from her face and studied the ruined silk bonnet with misgiving. The water stains would never come out of the silk. Her kid slippers were soaked as well.

She set the bonnet aside and made sure her hair was still rolled into a neat chignon at the back of her head.

"Your nose has a drop of water on its tip," Eddie said with ruthless candor and wiped his own nose with the back of his hand.

Justine wiped her nose on a damp handkerchief retrieved from her reticule and gave him a smile that held a hint of threat. "If you mention such uncouth details to your grandmother, she'll take the strap to your backside. She expects good manners in a young gentleman."

"But I'm not a young man, yet," Eddie said with annoying truthfulness.

"Here, drink your milk," Justine said and thrust the glass at him.

He shed the blanket and eagerly set to work on the pie. Currant juice dribbled down his chin, and he wore a rapt expression as he chewed.

As Justine waited for her tea, she noticed water dripping from the cloak onto the floor. She took the cloak to the door and shook it vigorously outside. The rain had slowed, but the sky still had a dull pewter gray cast, so like a sullen autumn day, she thought.

She folded the cloak once more and noticed a small square shape in the pocket. Curious, she touched it. An urge to pry came over her, and she looked around the vestibule to see if anyone was watching her. The taproom was empty except for Eddie, who concentrated wholly on the pie. Mattie had gone to the outhouse.

No, she told herself, *you cannot go through Damien's pockets. It would be a crime or at least an intrusion on his privacy.* Even as her hand slipped into the large pocket, she berated herself but could not stop her rampant curiosity. She gripped the packet and pulled it out. Same size as the one she'd found in the valise, she thought. This was wrapped in waterproof oilcloth and tied securely with a string.

Money? she wondered. Holding her breath, she clamped the cloak under her arm and quickly untied the string. Inside was a packet of letters written in French. She knew Damien's writing style, and this was different. Opening one letter, she looked at the signature, a stranger, a Frenchman.

A foreign spy?

Icy suspicion gripped her. What did these mean? She looked at the wrapping, but there was no address or any indication that the letters were going farther than Damien's pocket. The signature was that of a man, so they could not be letters from a French paramour, she deduced.

As she heard the sound of hooves on the lane, she wrapped the packet with clumsy hands, tied it with some difficulty, and slid it back into the pocket. Mayhap she should have taken them and shown them to Henry later. . . . No, Damien would have known they had been stolen, and he would suspect her of the crime.

As soon as they returned to Milverly, she would have to confide in Henry. The thought made her heart clench with despair. If Damien was a spy, all hope of a future with him was gone.

That realization brought forth the truth that, in the depths of her heart, she had harbored a hope that he would come back into her life.

She hid the cloak behind her as soon as she saw Damien with Agnes in the saddle. Shadwell came close behind with the carriage horses. The coachman and the groom came trudging not far behind.

She hurried to place the cloak over the chair where she'd fetched it.

Damien entered, his clothes dripping wet. Justine fought an urge to escape from his scrutiny. She took shelter by the tea tray that the host brought and busied herself with pouring four cups. She could sense Damien looking at her, but she did not return his glance.

"There you are, Eddie," Damien said. "You didn't dissolve into a puddle from the rain then?"

Eddie snorted a laugh and went to hug Damien's waist. "No. If I had, I would have run with the rain into the ocean."

Damien ruffled Eddie's hair, and Justine noted the genuine affection in his eyes. "I hear you let out my namesake."

"He never *moved*. Only lay there getting fat. The toads are more interesting."

"I hear you're raising a whole colony of them."

"Yes, the Milverly Toads. They are going to be the biggest and the bestest toads in all of Sussex."

"Don't bore Lord Lewington, Eddie," Nurse Mattie admonished as she shook the rain from her cloak. "We've heard more than we ever want to hear about toads."

Damien laughed. "At his age, I collected spiders in a box, and—"

"Have some tea while it's warm," Justine said sternly. "Eddie needs no more ideas for pets."

Eddie rushed back to his seat, and Damien lifted his cloak. Justine watched as he smoothed down the fabric as if subtly feeling for the packet.

She would not have thought anything of his movement if she hadn't seen the French letters. He folded the garment carefully and set it beside him on another chair. Probably cursing himself for forgetting he'd left her with the cloak or for being too polite to take it from her.

One thing was clear, the packet held great importance or he would not keep his cloak under such close guard.

Nine

"Will you accompany us to Enderby, Damien?" Eddie asked and wiped the crumbs from his mouth with the handkerchief his nurse gave him.

Damien shook his head. "No, my whelp . . . and more is the pity," he added as he gave Justine a searching glance.

"Aw, you could teach me how to use dueling pistols."

Damien pinched Eddie's chin and gazed at him sternly. "You're much too young for that sort of sport. Besides, your grandmother would have my ears strung up if I let you touch a weapon."

"Grandmama is not very violent. I don't think she would touch your ears," Eddie said with much confidence. "But if you're not coming with us, where are you going?"

Damien's jaw tightened, and Justine got a fleeting impression of his discomfort.

"Not that it's any of your business, but I'm headed to Crawley on business."

Crawley! Justine thought, where she'd found the valise.

"Can I come with you?"

"That's enough, Eddie!" said the nurse. "Not another word from you or your father will hear about your impudence from more people than myself. Come here."

Eddie squirmed but finally obeyed. He gave a wide yawn.

Justine suspected he would fall asleep before much longer.

She exchanged a glance with Damien, so many questions lying between them. She averted her face, unable to think of anything but the packet in his cloak pocket.

"I daresay we owe you our gratitude, Lord Lewington," she said formally. "But we can manage from here. Shadwell is arranging another conveyance as we speak. Please don't feel that you have to stay here for our sake. The rain has let up."

"It gives me great pleasure to stay here"—he leaned over the table out of earshot from the servants—"gazing at your beautiful face, Justine."

She fidgeted under his caressing evaluation, fearing her body's eager response to his admiration. It would not do to fall under his spell again. Especially after today, after finding more evidence that he was involved in treason against his country. She shuddered with unease.

"Are you cold?"

"No, just shivery from the damp weather," she replied in a thin voice. "Truly, let us not detain you."

He studied her for a long moment, and she sensed his reluctance to leave. Gathering his cloak under his arm, he stood. "Very well, your silent rejection speaks loud enough."

He bowed formally and nodded to the servants. "I pray you arrive at your destination without more mishaps."

He took with him the excitement, the very life in the room, and Justine suffered from the loss. She realized she would always miss him when he wasn't present. The thought disturbed her so much she almost cried.

Enderby, the main seat of Henry's family, an Elizabethan mansion of honey-colored stone, with arcaded buildings arranged around the forecourt, sat in a hollow surrounded by hills. Groomed rolling parkland and clusters of willow and ash, gave a softness to the estate, which brooded behind a brick wall. Visitors rode or drove through a gatehouse, and were presented a view of the arches framing the front entrance.

"We're here!" Eddie cried and rubbed the sleep from his eyes.

The clouds hung low and threatening over the valley; the air lay still and waiting, but it did not rain.

"Yes, and I expect you to behave," Mattie admonished. "Don't shout at your grandmother, and be sure to kiss her gently on her cheek. No big wrenching hugs."

Eddie pouted, but did not argue. He hung out the window with an expression of anticipation.

Feeling out of sorts, Justine gathered her things, and Agnes tried to brush the ruined bonnet. Justine wished she could shake off her despondent thoughts, but she kept seeing the packet of letters in Damien's pocket. *Dear God, where would it all end?*

Diana, the Dowager Countess Allenson, a short thin woman with proud bearing and a sprightly step greeted them on the front steps. "There you are, young man," she cried in pleasure as Eddie hopped out of the carriage as soon as it halted.

Eddie bowed as told and pecked the old woman's cheek. She wore a gray gown in the simple empire style, with long sleeves and a small ruffled white collar at the neck. A cap covered her graying hair, and her skin had the look of old wrinkled paper. Her brown eyes, however, sparkled like those of a young girl.

Justine's steps echoed on the brick forecourt as she hurried up the front steps to greet her hostess. Henry and Nora would live here one day but preferred to live at the smaller estate of Milverly to keep their privacy.

"Justine, you look lovelier than ever," the dowager said. "A season in London has given you town polish, and your gown is very smart."

"You're flattering me, Lady Allenson," Justine said and kissed the dry cheek.

"Do dispense with formalities, dear child. Call me Diana. We're in the country now and don't have to stand on ceremony. Come in." She led the way, her arm draped over Eddie's sturdy shoulder.

A square hallway had mahogany staircases on both sides.

They met above at a landing whose walls had been decorated with painted figures of Greek gods and goddesses. Marble statues of goddesses in flowing chitons guarded the staircases on both sides, and urns filled with flowers gave warmth to the formality of the ancient building. Justine knew from past visits that doors led to a library on one side, a dining room, and a large drawing room. On the other side, two salons, where visitors were entertained.

"You can go up and refresh yourself before dinner, but after that I want to hear all the gossip from Milverly."

Honest and direct to a fault, Justine thought with a smile.

Shadwell came up and bowed. "Lady Allenson, do you need me further, or am I free to return to Milverly? There's much work."

Lady Allenson studied the gentleman from head to toe. "And deprive me of a young person's witty company? Tsk, tsk, I daresay my son can get along without you for a few days."

"I—" the secretary began, but the dowager interrupted him.

"Nonsense! I rattle around in this old house with only the servants for company most of the time. Don't deprive me of this simple pleasure."

Shadwell flushed. He averted his gaze and withdrew, his gait slightly stiff.

"He's rather zealous in his work, but Henry said he could stay here until it's time to go back," Justine explained. "Shadwell probably feels it's his duty—"

"I don't want to hear it. A week's respite won't hurt him, rather the opposite I should say. I will dispatch a note to Henry."

"Henry's work is very important. Perhaps Shadwell feels trapped here," Justine said feebly, but Diana only shook her head.

"He needs a few days reprieve." She clapped her hands. "Dinner will be precisely at seven. Since it is your first day here, young Eddie, you shall dine with us tonight."

Eddie leaped with delight, almost knocking over a

Chinese vase that must have been worth a small fortune. Mattie compressed her lips and hauled the boy upstairs.

"So much energy," the dowager mused aloud. "And so like Henry when he was a child." She sighed. "Where have all the years gone?"

Later, Justine divulged every piece of gossip that she could remember, carefully avoiding the subject of Lord Lewington. "We will soon have news of Nora's situation," she said finally, as her thoughts returned to her sister's ordeal. "Eddie might have a brother or sister by now."

They found out about the baby late that evening as a messenger arrived with the news. Henry had dispatched one of the grooms with the glad tidings, but it was Damien Trowbridge who walked in as Diana and Justine were having a cup of cocoa in the drawing room before going upstairs. A sinking feeling settled in Justine's stomach as she viewed his tall powerful frame in the door opening.

"Good evening, ladies," he said with a lazy grin. "I hope I'm not intruding?"

The dowager countess threw up her thin hand in surprise. Her eyes widened with pleasure, and her mouth fell open. "Good heavens, Damien! Come here, you rogue." She patted the space beside her on the sofa. "It's been an age since I saw you."

Damien strolled across the room, his gait sinuous like that of a cat. Justine's heart pounded wildly, and her throat became dry. She set down her cup with a trembling hand.

"Damien," she murmured, as he leaned over the Diana's outstretched hand. "What are you doing here?" she added in a louder voice.

"I do own one of the fastest horses in the area, and I know many paths over the hills. I come with the wonderful news that Henry and Nora have been blessed with a healthy baby girl. She was born three hours ago."

Justine could not hide the tears of delight filling her eyes, and Diana wiped at the corners of hers. The older woman spread her arms.

"How splendid! This calls for a celebration, don't you

think? Damien, please pull the bell ropes. Radbert shall
bring in the finest brandy, and we shall make a toast."

Radbert, the decrepit Enderby butler, brought in a dusty
bottle from the cellars. He uncorked it gingerly and poured
three glasses with a gentle hand.

"Ah! An ancient bottle of the finest French brandy put by
for occasions like these. Old Melville, my husband, stocked
his cellars well. They are a constant reminder of him and his
thoughtfulness," the dowager said, her voice trembling with
emotion.

Radbert brought around the tray with glasses, then left.

Diana raised her glass. "To the new child. Let her live
long and happily."

The brandy, smooth yet burning, slid down Justine's
throat, and she felt as if the new child had been truly blessed
and welcomed by these fond relatives. The good news had
brought elation as well, and Justine's mind had for once
been removed from the nagging thoughts of her everyday
life. The brandy helped her to keep floating on a cloud of
bliss.

"I wonder what they are going to name her," the dowager
said and then drank the last of the brandy in her glass.

"Probably Diana." Damien turned to Justine, his gaze a
velvet caress on her face. "What is your mother's name?
You never told me."

"Alexandra Beatrice Honoria Justine," she replied, smiling as his face fell at her recitation of the long list. "Father
calls her Alexa."

The dowager crowed. "Diana Alexandra, I daresay."

"Or Alexandra Diana," Damien said with a devious grin.
"It depends who has the stronger will."

The dowager swatted his arm. "You're incorrigible!
Henry does, of course." Her gaze traveled from Damien to
Justine. "Are you going back to Ardmore Crest tonight,
Damien?"

"No . . . I have taken a room at the George in the
village. Thought I'd take advantage of your good nature.
I'm hoping for a breakfast invitation tomorrow—"

"Only breakfast?" Diana's eyebrows lifted. "If you've

come this far, you might as well stay for dinner as well. I shall have three young people to entertain me since Shadwell is not leaving."

Damien grinned. "I am delighted to accept."

The dowager hid a yawn behind her hand. "I shall sit here and savor the moment. Why don't you two young people take a stroll on the terrace?" She craned her neck to glance out the window. "I believe the moon is out between the storms."

"Are you trying to get rid of me?" Justine asked with a laugh.

"No . . . I just think you should have a moment to talk. Keeping me company must be tiresome. To look at the stars with an exciting young gentleman must be ever so much more inspiring."

"It wouldn't be the first time we've looked at the stars," Damien murmured.

"Good! Go then, remind yourselves that there is romance, not only tedious chores."

Justine hesitated, but Damien held out his arm toward her. Short of being rude, she couldn't reject him. She set down her glass and followed him through the long open French windows that served as doors to the terrace.

"I'd rather look at the stars in your eyes than the ones in the sky," he said. "It has been a long time since I saw a twinkle in your lovely eyes."

"There has been no reason to twinkle," she said tartly. "I am not taken in by gentlemen's blandishments any longer, and they certainly do not put stars in my eyes." She glanced at him quickly. "So don't take credit for my happiness. I'm simply delighted that Nora is safe and the baby is healthy."

"Eddie won't like the idea of a sister," he said. "At that age, girls are naught but a nuisance."

"They are a nuisance at any age, wouldn't you say?" she whispered.

"I can think of ways to amuse myself with gir—ladies. I do prefer the ladies, especially one lady, who has shown she wants nothing to do with me." He stopped and put his hand to her cheek, his fingers caressing the nape of her neck.

Justine moved away, but his presence made it difficult for her to maintain her resolve to avoid him at all costs.

He shifted closer, and she found it hard to breathe as he looked deeply into her eyes. Moonlight glittered in his, and an unspoken challenge.

"I know you're not wholly indifferent to my charms, Justine. Why are you holding back? I have shown my desire to pursue what we left behind in London, to start over. I can't promise that our attraction is strong enough to push aside the doubts—your doubts about my honor, my doubts that true love exists."

He spoke candidly, his face open, almost begging her to accept his offer. She weighed his words, feeling her love like a painful burden as she could not share it with him. Not as long as the questions about his involvement in the spying went unanswered. But how could she confront him without raising his ire? Should she confront him with her knowledge of the valise and the letters? If she challenged him, he might turn against her. The thought frightened her, for she knew a stormy temper lurked under the smooth gentlemanly facade. She would not know how to handle herself if he turned against her.

"I can see you retreat behind a mask of politeness, Justine." He touched her cheek gently, pulling a velvet fingertip down to the corner of her mouth. "Don't be afraid of me."

She hesitated, and he swept her into his arms and crushed her against him. The solid body, the strength of him, made her lose her will to fight.

She lifted her face to his, and he touched her lips, a mere brush of his. A thrill shot down her spine, and she clung to him as he kissed her hard, ravished her senses, touching her soul as his tongue caressed hers.

He let go of her reluctantly, still holding her arms as he gazed deeply into her eyes.

"You know exactly how to seduce the ladies, with smooth words and dizzying kisses," she said breathlessly. She wished desperately that this kiss had been the beginning of a new, more trusting relationship with him, but the doubts lingered like a poison fog in her chest. "I'm not sure my father would approve of your behavior; in fact, I know he wouldn't."

He pulled his mouth into a grimace. "You're right. Your father would have my head on a platter. I have taken advantage of you, and right under the nose of the dowager."

She could not help but smile. "You have never missed an opportunity for dalliance."

That brought out an answering smile. "That is the prerogative of a rake. Seduction of damsel and chaperone alike."

Stung by his careless words, she pulled away. "Yes . . . how right you are. I forget sometimes."

"Because some part of you believes in me and cherishes me."

She nodded, choking on her emotions. "But I'm not a naive fool any longer. I am immune to your flattery."

He lowered his arms, which he'd held open as an invitation. "Naive you are not, but as lovely and desirable as ever."

"Oh, Damien, I have nothing else to say. It has to end here, *has to,* as it began in London—with you flattering me. Good night and sweet dreams." She moved abruptly toward the open French window where a curtain swayed in the gentle breeze. The dowager sat on the couch, her head tilting forward as she dozed. Justine touched her shoulder.

"I'm going up to bed, Diana. Good night."

The dowager glanced toward the window with a dazed look. "Where's Damien?"

"I'd say he went to seek his bed at the George."

The dowager smile. "I do like that rogue so very much." She wound her arm through Justine's as they left the room together.

"Do you trust him—really trust him?"

"Hmm, I don't know him well enough to say, but I sense that he's basically an honorable man despite his reputation as a rake."

"Why would you say that? Do you know something the rest of society does not?"

Diana gave another yawn behind her hand. "I have a lifetime of experience, and I trust my own judgment. Damien is a good man, even if he had a rather loveless childhood. His father was a truly heartless scoundrel. I daresay Damien grew up and made his own choices, none of them based upon the poor values he inherited from his father. Damien has a sharp head on his shoulders."

"Yes, I've noticed." *Except for the fact that he's involved in illegal activities,* Justine thought.

Ten

SHADWELL SHARED BREAKFAST with Justine and the dowager countess. He gave Justine sideways thoughtful looks during the meal and glowered at Damien as Radbert showed him in. Justine wondered what the secretary had against Damien.

Damien wore buckskins, a striped silk waistcoat, and a coat of black superfine. The crisp linen contrasted handsomely with his sun-bronzed skin, and his smile could have charmed the most reluctant heart. It set Justine's teeth on edge even as her heart pounded with longing.

She stubbornly refused to be drawn out as Damien lifted his eyebrows in a gesture of amused challenge. Shadwell gave the marquess another glowering look. The only person who chirped with delight was the dowager.

"I'm pleased you decided to pay us a visit before returning to Oldhaven, Damien. You have the knack for cheering up an old soul."

Damien kissed Diana's cheek. "I have to put to good use the charm the gods gave me," he drawled, "or 'twill be wasted."

Diana crowed and swatted his arm. "You rascal!" She waved at the butler. "Radbert, bring in more coffee, and make sure His Lordship is served from all the chafing dishes

on the sideboard. I like to watch young men eat. Such hardy
appetites, such enjoyment of food."

Damien sent an amused glance at Shadwell, but Justine
sensed the secretary's reluctance to respond. His evident
dislike hung around him like a mist. He shot her a guilty
glance as if feeling her scrutiny. His cheeks reddened, and
he fidgeted with the fork on his plate. She could not explain
why, but she sensed he was hiding something. Mayhap the
feeling rose from his reserved manner and stilted conversation.

Damien sat down across from Justine, giving her a warm
enveloping smile that could as easily have been a real
embrace.

"Has Eddie planted any hairy creatures in your bed yet,
Lady Allenson?" he asked while accepting a plate of ham
and eggs from the footman serving the meal.

Diana chuckled. "No . . . but I daresay it's only a
matter of time before Eddie instigates some form of
mischief. He runs his poor nurse ragged. I heard her scold
him on the stairs at dawn."

Damien cut the slices of ham. "I'd like to take him for a
walk later if you don't mind."

"By all means, take him through the park and the spinney.
We can all benefit from a walk in this lovely weather,
especially Justine, who looks pale and peaked this morning."

Justine gave a small smile, but found it a strain. "If I look
tired, it's because of Eddie. I heard him on the stairs as well,
and I could not go back to sleep afterwards."

"To my discriminating gaze, you look lovely as always,
Miss Bryerly."

Diana gave another crow of laughter. "You're not one to
lack the admiration of the gentlemen, dear Justine, and I'd
say Damien has excellent taste."

Justine grew hotter with the dowager's every word, but
she tilted her chin up and gazed squarely at Damien. "He
has a speech designed to turn the heads of the ladies, and I
cannot approve of such deviousness."

Damien put down his fork, and a devilish smile played

around his mouth. "I daresay my words touched a tender spot. But Shadwell here does not ruffle your composure with flattery. Sensible fellow."

"At least when he opens his mouth, he speaks the truth—unlike some people I know." Justine smiled at the discomfited secretary and saw a flame of admiration leap to life in his eyes.

"Yes . . . I try to speak with honesty," he said. "But I don't have that many opportunities to converse with the ladies. My work is rather demanding—leaves little time for visiting friends."

"Romance is important while you're young and able to move around freely. You should take the opportunity to see everything. When one is as old as I am, riding is out of the question and a walk is rather difficult."

"I'm sure you have had your share of romance," Damien said and winked at the dowager. "I judge that by the merry twinkle in your eye. Even if your body is getting on, your heart is forever young."

Diana's twinkle grew brighter. "Yes . . . in my salad days, we took every opportunity to entertain ourselves. Endless balls and masquerades, picnics, and card parties. I was a giddy young thing, always ready for a lark. When I met Melville, all that ended, but I didn't miss the gatherings. I had found the gentleman who could give me all I needed. He fulfilled my life."

"That is an endearing story," Justine said and patted her mouth with a napkin. The revelations touched a tender spot in her heart and provoked a feeling of embarrassment, but the dowager did not seem to be mortified in the slightest.

The dowager tilted her head to one side. "Once you find the person who can touch your heart, you don't need anyone else for happiness."

Silence filled the room, and Justine pondered the older woman's words. Should she give in to her overwhelming feelings for the marquess despite the danger? How could she be sure that he would turn out as kind and loving as Melville must have been? She couldn't be sure. Anyhow, she would not bare her feelings to a traitor.

"Miss Bryerly, would you like to take a stroll after breakfast?" Shadwell asked, his gaze intent on her face.

"That would be a pleasure," she said. She rose, as did the gentlemen. "I shall go upstairs and see that Eddie is ready to go out. Won't be a minute."

The dowager countess wore a fringed shawl over her pearl gray gown and carried an unfurled parasol to protect her face from the sun. Justine carried one as well but was less severely dressed in a white dimity gown with short puff sleeves and kid gloves. A straw bonnet with green ribbons protected her hair.

Shadwell fell into step beside her on the path winding through the Enderby park. "I must say I'm enjoying a few days away from the endless letter writing," he said with a wry smile. "Your brother-in-law is a stern taskmaster, and the matters of England are never finished."

"Everyone is entitled to rest now and then. Henry can't crack his whip here. Even he has to obey the commands of his mother, Lady Allenson."

Shadwell studied her, and she felt the force of his gaze. A shrewd personality hid behind that stiffly polite exterior. "I confess I'm delighted to spend that time with you, Miss Bryerly. I also confess I've admired you from afar since I arrived at Milverly."

Justine twirled her parasol, suddenly at a loss for words. Unprepared for his admiration, she'd only seen him in the role of Henry's reserved secretary. "You flatter me, Mr. Shadwell."

"You are an exceptional woman, if I may be so bold. I know we don't move in the same circles and that I have little hope of gaining your attention, let alone affection. I cannot expect an inheritance, and my means are very modest, too modest to offer a great lady. However, I have noticed your sadness, and I reveal my admiration in hope that it will raise your spirits. Not for any other reason. I do not expect you to look upon me beyond friendship."

"You are acting like a gentleman." *Unlike others I know.*

She gave Damien's back a dour look as he walked with the dowager.

"I cannot conceive of acting in any other way." His mouth twisted in a bitter grimace. "I wish there was a way for me—that I could speak of romance, but my older brother has made sure I cannot have a future other than one in service. I don't resent my work, but I resent that my brother would get everything and refuses to support our sister. You see, she's an invalid."

"I am sorry to hear that. Who is looking after her?"

"An elderly aunt. I support them while my brother—" He stopped abruptly, evidently thinking he was revealing too much of himself.

They walked along in silence, Justine pondering his words. "Life is never fair."

Shadwell gave a convulsive shake of the head but did not pursue the topic.

Eddie jumped and skipped ahead, bouncing in a mud puddle, ruining his breeches. His neckcloth hung askew and sported grass spots, and his hair stood straight up. In his hand, he carried a twig, with which he whipped any tall blade of grass in his path.

"Do be careful, Eddie. If you get back covered with mud, Mattie will give you a severe scolding," Justine said, "and she will put you to bed without supper."

Damien lifted the child up in the air, and Eddie squealed, waving his arms as if he were flying. "When I was your age," Damien said, "my nurse would have taken the strap to my backside for getting mud on my clothes."

"I'm sure there are scars," the dowager said with an evil laugh.

Shadwell frowned disapprovingly. "I'm appalled that the marquess would use such a *word,* in the presence of ladies—and a child," he said under his breath.

Justine could have informed him that the marquess did exactly as he pleased without asking for anyone else's opinions. "I'll pretend I wasn't listening," she said, entertained against her wishes by the marquess's bold vocabulary. He had a deft hand with children. Eddie's presence seemed to lift the burden of problems from Damien's shoulders. He looked years younger as he raced the small boy to the gate.

They kept walking under the shade of stately oaks. A cool breeze blew among the branches, and the sky had darkened ominously along the horizon. Justine sighed. "Looks like more rain to come. The ground is already saturated."

"Yes, the local farmers speak of disaster. Any more rain, and the crops are bound to fail."

Damien hooted in the distance, and Eddie's shrill laughter rose among the trees. The dowager chuckled and walked with surprisingly spry steps to join them.

"Tell me, Miss Bryerly," said Shadwell, "you know the marquess rather well, don't you?"

Justine felt heat rise in her cheeks at the probing question. "I know him well enough, I should say. Well enough to—" She did not pursue the words aloud. *Well enough to stay away from him,* she had planned to say, but it was untrue. She couldn't stay away from him, or he from her, it seemed.

He constantly turned up on her path. The thought warmed her, yet worried her more than she could admit.

"Miss Bryerly, if I may be frank, we're searching for a . . . a, well, treacherous spy in Oldhaven, someone who is knowledgeable enough to deal with the French. A turncoat, someone who sells information to the French while working for the British government." He slanted her a searching glance. "I daresay Lord Allenson would disapprove if he knew that I'm divulging this to you, but I have been hoping for some help, a clue to the identity of the villain."

"You think Lord Lewington is spying for the French?" she asked breathlessly. Her throat felt so tight with worry that she imagined she might never breathe again. Thinking of the valise, she slowed her step. Her gaze traveled to Damien. She heard his sunny laughter and his teasing voice. Should she bare her suspicious thoughts to Shadwell? A gentleman dedicated to his work, he would immediately investigate her find. The thought of Damien shamed, ruined by treason, turned her blood to ice.

But she had to confide in someone.

No, not Shadwell, she thought, even as the words hung on her tongue. She liked to share her worries, but a part of her had to protect Damien from upset and pain. *Shadwell could very well strike fast, slash apart Damien's life with one swift stroke—accusation. Perhaps he would revel in it . . .* The thought pressed upon her, and she had to curb an urge to flee from the man's probing gaze.

"You must be mistaken," she said lightly. "Lord Lewington took part in the war against the French. He would not consider turning against his country." She stiffened her back. "Truly, I'm appalled that you would entertain such destructive suspicions, Mr. Shadwell."

He sniffed. "I suspect anyone and all until the traitor is caught." He let out a deep sigh as if he'd held his breath for a long time. "But I am a complete bore to speak about this while we're enjoying a walk in the country. Very uncouth of me."

"I'm flattered that you would think I could help," she said noncommittally.

He gave a tight smile, and she sensed he was trying hard to relax. "I would not want you to think badly of me, Miss Bryerly. I would be sad to discover—"

"Say no more, Mr. Shadwell. I'm sure you mean well, and are only doing your duty."

He relaxed visibly, and his smile enlivened his stern face. They joined the others, and even though anguished about being close to Damien, she was relieved to move away from Shadwell. She linked her arm to Diana's.

"Is Eddie bothering you with his chatter?"

"No, my dear, he's bringing me back to life! When I'm alone, I nod off on the sofa in the drawing room. I need scoundrels like Eddie—and Damien—to keep me young."

Eddie swung on the wooden gate, his feet tucked between the two lowest planks. Damien pushed the gate from one side to the other. "Do it again, Damien!" Eddie shouted every time Damien made a move to stop the game. "Again!"

"That's enough, Eddie," Damien said at last and pulled

the boy away from the gate. "Your grandmother will have your hide if you destroy her property."

Eddie went willingly enough, rushing ahead of everyone else. Shadwell hurried after him, and Damien fell into step beside Justine.

"You have a good hand with Eddie," she said. "You're a different person when playing with him." Mayhap Damien's character wasn't wholly tarnished by past debauchery and womanizing. She knew the truth as if it had sprung from the very core of herself. Her knees weakened, and her heart raced as she glimpsed that sudden hope. He had changed. He wasn't beyond redemption. A libertine would not have the time to enjoy playing tag with a child in a summer meadow.

"He entertains me, reminds me of my own childhood."

Knowing his childhood had not been as happy as that of Eddie, Justine glanced at Damien. A cloud came over his features, and at the same time, heavy gray clouds obscured the sun. A strange brooding air fell over the park.

The dowager muttered to herself and looked at the lowering sky. She clucked her tongue in dismay. "The rain is back, and it's not a single storm. We'll be drenched if we don't go back."

As if the servants had read her thoughts, a chaise and pair moved toward them at a great clip. The dowager countess's coachman halted the horses and turned the carriage around on the lane with difficulty.

"It's not raining yet," Damien said. "Eddie and Diana can ride back with that sour-faced secretary. You and I could walk back. It's not far, and I would have a chance to spend time with you alone without a chaperone hanging on every word."

Tempted, Justine felt as if she was teetering on a dangerous crest. She shook her head.

"No. It's out of the question."

She'd rather be safe than bleeding from a broken heart at the bottom of the ravine of romantic dalliance. Running, she caught up with Diana before Damien had time to protest. Her heart hammered almost painfully in her chest. It was no use denying it; she had fallen in love with Damien all over again—that is, if she had fallen out of love at all. She could not delude herself any longer. The truth had crashed upon her, loud and clamoring. *Love.* With a deep sigh, she looked out the window as the coach lumbered back to Enderby.

Damien stood in the lane staring at her, a stricken expression on his face. She had saved herself from falling at the last moment, but would she be safe the next time she came across the dangerous Lord Lewington? One day she might break down and confess the true state of her heart to him, and then she would verily be lost.

Eleven

Damien had tried to get close to Justine, to no avail. Like a shadow, she flitted away the moment he entered the room or pursued her in a hallway at Enderby.

He ought to go home, not make a fool of himself here where he wasn't wanted. He might as well admit the truth: he'd lost Justine the moment he'd left her in London. His fear had made him shy away from her, and now it was too late to mend the rift. It was always *too late* for him, he thought, grimacing. His sordid past would hunt him to the end of his days.

Standing on the front steps of the Enderby house, he massaged his neck as a headache started pounding in his skull. The damned heavy weather was to blame. It had rained for days, and it kept on raining. Everything held a patina of dampness, and the smell of mildew hung in every house he entered, be it mansion or the humble tavern in the village.

Diana received him in the drawing room. Water sluiced against the windowpanes; its glittery streaks held no suggestion of summer and heat. *Could be autumn,* he thought glumly, then tried to shake himself out of his dour mood.

"You're still moping about here then, Damien? How

many days have passed now without your getting any closer to the desire of your heart?" she asked, blunt as usual.

"I don't know what you're talking about," he said more stiffly than he'd planned.

"Ha! You can't fool an old woman. I have seen everything, several times over. You're enamored of darling Justine, and don't say that you aren't, because it stands written all over your face."

Damien could not quite smile. "That obvious, is it?"

"That obvious." She tapped a gnarled finger on the window. "I'm tired of this weather, Damien. Take me away to Egypt, Turkey, or wherever the sun resides."

"I wish I could," he replied, this time smiling as her abrasive voice cheered him up. "We could make it our honeymoon."

"Dear me, what a totty-headed idea!" She laughed nevertheless. She gazed at him intently, her eyes old and wise in the muted light from the window. "Hmm, a rather attractive one at that. Wish that I were forty years younger. I would snap you up in a trice, not act all missish like Justine."

"Please don't berate—"

She left him no time to finish his sentence as she pushed her hand against his chest. "I know!" she said in high spirits. "You might escort me to Milverly so that I can inspect my new grandchild."

"A capital idea, Diana."

"I know I haven't been invited, but I'll drive over with the pretext of delivering Justine safely back to Milverly." Her eyes danced with suppressed excitement. "And you, young whippersnapper, shall escort us both. I'll send Shadwell ahead to announce our arrival. He's been sniffing around Justine much too closely. We can't have that!"

"I agree completely," Damien said, and clenched his jaw.

"Go now . . . go back to the George and pack. Return in three hours. We'll be waiting for you, the traveling chaise laden with trunks."

"Are you going to make it a lengthy stay?" Damien

asked, wondering how long Henry would suffer his parent's peremptory presence.

"Long enough to see you walk down the aisle with the lady of your heart," Diana said and raised a mutinous chin.

Damien shook his head in wonder and betook himself down to the village. When he returned, the traveling coach was indeed laden with trunks, and servants darted back and forth carrying bandboxes and portmanteaux.

There was no sign of Shadwell, but Damien noticed a flash of blue silk gown and a wobbling ostrich feather by the front door. Justine. Her anger and frustration came like a palpable wave across the front lawn even before he could clearly see her expression. Perhaps she had difficulty accepting Diana's abrupt change of plans, and he knew for certain that Justine would not approve of having his presence thrust upon her during the trip to Milverly.

He smiled. This time she would not be able to run away from him.

Milverly could have been located at the north end of Scotland for all the time it took to drive the short distance. Rain pelted the carriage roof incessantly, a monotonous drumming that gave Justine an urge to scream with frustration. Especially since she had to endure Damien's searching glances. Sometimes he looked at her with a mocking gleam in his eyes as if he found her wanting, unable to understand something he had already understood with ease. Thank goodness the dowager was present to alleviate the tension or Justine might have jumped out of the carriage in a fit of exasperation.

She drew a sigh of relief as the coach rolled up the drive to Milverly. Without waiting for the assistance of a footman, she stepped out, leaving Damien's disturbing presence behind as she ran into the house.

Henry came down the stairs as she started up. "There you are, dear," he said with a smile. "You look like you've missed us all. Is that the reason for your hurry?"

Justine gave him a hug. "Henry, how is my sister?"

"She's as rosy as a rose, happy and well." He pinched her

chin and stared at her intently. "Is there something the matter? You look peaked?"

She shook her head. "No . . . but I'm glad to be back. Eddie was running me ragged, but your mother enjoyed his company. By the way, Diana came with us."

Henry's face fell, but before he had a chance to bemoan this new turn of events, she said, "Now I have to see Nora and my new niece."

Henry wore the expression of a long-suffering martyr as he stepped downstairs. Justine stifled a laugh behind her hand. *How could anyone not enjoy Diana's company?* she wondered as she knocked at the door and stepped into Nora's bedchamber.

Nora's fact lit up. "Darling sis! How delightful that you've returned. I feared you would continue on to Bath without coming back here first."

"I would not go without welcoming my niece." Justine saw the bundle in Nora's arms and hurried to the bedside. Out of the folds of a fringed white blanket stared a pair of perfectly round blue eyes. Pink fat cheeks, a sweet button mouth, an endearing nose, tiny ears, and a tuft of dark hair completed the face of the new baby.

"She's simply adorable," Justine said and touched her fingertip to one downy cheek. "Oh, Nora. You must be so proud." She kissed her sister on the forehead, noting that Nora looked happier than ever before.

"I am proud." She lifted the baby, and the small face crumpled into a huge yawn.

"Look at that mouth!"

"She has a pair of lungs fit for a boy," Nora said with a small grimace. "She screams louder than Eddie did at the same age." She glanced around Justine. "Where is my scamp? I've missed him."

"He's with his grandmother downstairs. Henry went to greet them."

Nora chuckled. "Diana? Well, this is grand. A regular family reunion." She gave the bundle of squirming child to Justine. "Hold her for a minute while I find a more demure wrap." She blushed and threw Justine a guilty glance.

"Henry likes this wrap, nothing but a wisp of spiderweb and lace."

Justine had some difficulty picturing Henry's adoration, but the thought of their intimacy made her hot with embarrassment. As she cradled the baby and crooned, she wondered about Damien's tastes in female wraps. Would his eyes darken with interest if he saw her in a . . . She couldn't complete the thought; it disturbed her more than any of his intimate glances had. God, why couldn't she forget him, put him out of her mind? He wouldn't leave her alone, that's why.

Nora tidied her appearance with a demure velvet wrapping gown and stuffed her hair under a lace-edged cap, now the picture of a lovely matron. Childbearing became Nora, put a wonderful bloom of happiness on her appearance.

Henry knocked on the door just as Justine gave the baby back to her sister. "Are you presentable?" he asked. "Mother won't wait another minute to see the child, and Damien is kicking his heels in the hallway."

"Show them up," Nora said with supreme confidence.

Justine sat down next to her sister. The dowager countess entered, her arms wide to embrace Nora and the newcomer. They cooed and twittered over that small soft face in the blankets, and Henry exchanged an amused glance with Justine.

"Silly women," he mouthed to her, and she made a face in defense of the female gender.

Damien entered with less pomp, Eddie clinging to his neck. The two surveyed the scene, and Damien's gaze fell on Justine. It told of intimacy, of promise that he could give her a family of her own.

Heat rose in her cheeks, and she glanced to the floor.

"Mama! Is that my new sister?" Eddie shouted and wiggled out of Damien's arms. He raced to the chair where Nora sat and hugged her fiercely. Then he glanced at the rosy baby face. "Zounds, but she's ugly!" he exclaimed.

Nora frowned. "Where have you learned such an uncouth expression?"

"Damien says it all the time," Eddie replied with great

confidence. "She's so small, nothing but a doll," he added in disgust.

"She shouts louder than you already, so you'd better be careful to keep your derogatory comments to yourself," Henry said.

Eddie touched his sister's cheek thoughtfully, while leaning heavily against Nora. "I'll wager she doesn't like toads," he said at last.

Everyone laughed. Damien stepped forward to admire the baby. "What are you going to name her?"

Henry gave his mother's back a long stare, and Justine could barely sustain her mirth. "Diana?" she asked.

Henry nodded vigorously. "Diana Alexandra Justine," he said.

The dowager countess straightened her back and beamed with pleasure. "I daresay you still have an ounce of respect for your old mother," she said to Henry. "Diana is not a bad name. It's strong. A female needs a strong name to get on in this world."

Henry laughed and went to order champagne. The air seemed to bubble with happiness, and Justine noticed that Damien was quieter than usual, withdrawn and pensive. He stood by the window looking at the gray, sullen sky.

Something squeezed her heart painfully, as if reminding her that she had to let go of a burden before it was too late. That burden was distrust and suspicion. And the valise.

God, let him be innocent, let the valise belong to someone else. Praying should have helped, but it only made her more miserable.

Damien stared at the approaching new storm, the masses of cloud so heavy with rain they hung on the very treetops. *It is raining outside, and it's raining in my heart,* he thought. All along the trip to Milverly, he'd tried to find a way through Justine's armor, but she'd only crept more deeply into her defense.

Having seen Nora's new child, a fierce longing had come over him for children of his own. It was time, but he had to prove he could put all of his sordid past behind him before he could win Justine's love. He threw a glance over his shoulder, catching her looking at him. Misery and suspicion, mayhap a hint of anger in that look. It pained him so much he could not remain in the room to receive any more disapproving glances from her. Her continuing rejection had whipped him long enough.

He would start anew by sending his mistress packing. He should have done that a long time ago if he wanted to catch Justine's affection.

He strode across the room, gave the ladies a bow, and whispered to Henry, "Congratulations, old fellow. I'm so jealous I can't stay to celebrate, but I'll be back at another time—when I hope to call you my future brother-in-law." He slapped Henry's back and grinned at his friend's shocked expression.

"I say! Damien rushed off in a hurry," Henry said as the front door slammed below. He gave Justine a thoughtful glance. "Is there something I ought to know?"

She wondered what Damien had said to put that expression on Henry's face. But truly, she didn't want to know. What Damien said was none of her business. "No, nothing, Henry."

A week later Justine discovered that Damien's mistress had left Sussex. Oldhaven was always buzzing with gossip, and the servants at Milverly had relatives and friends who spread the latest news with great alacrity.

That *tart* at the Fisherman's Luck had taken her silk gowns and her gaudy hats and her replenished purse with her as she left Fairhaven. And good riddance! The marquess had no business carrying on with his light-skirts right under the noses of the godfearin' ladies of the parish, the rumor went.

Justine took avid interest in the gossip, for it involved the marquess. Part of her misery lifted, and that made it easier to endure Henry and Nora's happiness.

It was clear that Baby Diana had inherited the older Diana's forthright speech, and she voiced her opinion at any hour of the night and day. Eddie's suggestion that they stuff a mitten into the baby's mouth earned him a severe scolding.

Justine tried to cheer him up by paying the Milverly Toads a visit. They were inspecting the ugly creatures as the butler brought a letter to her.

"From Charity," she read as she spread the stiff paper on her lap. Sitting on a box in the shed by the pond, she read the letter:

Dear Justine,

I heard the good news of Nora's safe confinement. My felicitations to the family. (I have written to Nora to express my delight.) I surmise that you're free to throw yourself into a whirl of summer gatherings. I have persuaded Papa to sponsor a dance for me here at Jasmine Cottage on Friday evening. Mind you, it will be a small affair since there's not much room to dance, but my closest friends will all attend. I hope to receive a speedy confirmation that you can come. Please accept my invitation. My evening of entertainment would not be the same without you.

Your friend, Charity

Justine immediately thought of Damien. If he was going, she would not. She recalled, however, that Henry had mentioned that Damien had traveled up to London on business. *Spying business, no doubt,* Justine thought, but she immediately regretted her suspicion. If anything, Damien took good care of the estate business.

I will go. What Damien does should not direct my life, she said to herself as she watched Eddie stuffing a toad into his pocket. A water stain quickly marred the wool of his inexpressibles.

"Where are you taking that toad?" she asked and pushed the letter under her sash since she was not carrying her reticule.

Eddie gave her a guilty look, and his jaw took a mutinous angle. "I thought Baby Diana would like to see it."

Justine smiled, even though she'd planned to lecture him. "I doubt that Baby Diana will see the finer points, the elegance of your toad. She can barely focus her blue eyes, and I suspect that she would not want to make the toad's face her first memory of this world."

Eddie pouted.

"You have to admit that the toad is not the most handsome fellow you've ever seen. I think Baby Diana would rather see your face than its."

Eddie's eyes lit up. "You really think so?"

"I'm sure of it." She took his hand. "Come, let's go and find out."

Twelve

"You look lovely," Nora said as Justine, wearing a pale cream, watered silk ball gown, turned around in front of the mirror. "Such bloom in your cheeks."

Yes, mayhap I don't look like a pale tormented ghost any longer, Justine thought. Her spirits had improved since Charity's invitation. The sleeves puffed nicely on her slim arms, and the blue satin sash echoed the blue color of her eyes. The silk felt elegant and shimmered as she moved. She draped a gauzy lace shawl over her shoulders and tucked a stray curl under a pin. Blue silk flowers adorned her hair, and pearl earrings her ears.

She'd had a respite from Damien's provocative presence, and now she looked forward to a night of entertainment that he would not attend. Still, part of her could never forget him, part of her missed him.

The only problem nagging her was Damien's valise. If she accused him of treason to Henry or anyone else, his life—and hers—would never be the same again. He would be questioned and his life probed by the highest powers in the land. Did she have the courage to expose him and then live with the knowledge of his suffering? Perhaps she ought to warn him, show some faith in him. She should.

One moment she needed to make a clean breast of the

whole; another moment she swore she would keep the secret forever. Let the law find out if Damien was the man who sold secrets to the French. Why had she had the misfortune to find the valise in the first place? Fate kept tangling her life with Damien's in a most uncomfortable way.

"The carriage is waiting, Justine."

The drawing room at Jasmine Cottage had been adorned with arches of roses in the doorways and masses of candles in crystal chandeliers and polished silver candelabras. The men of the orchestra of violins, flutes, and pianoforte, arranged the music sheets. Footmen served glasses of refreshment, and Justine accepted a glass of ratafia from Hoppy, the rather forward friend of Roger Trowbridge.

"Dashed crush," he said, referring to the gathering of guests.

Hoppy looked elegant in buff pantaloons and a coat of dark blue velvet. He wore his starched neckcloth tied with flair and his shirt points very high. Still, there was something furtive about him tonight; he rarely looked her in the eyes. He kept staring at the door.

"Are you expecting anyone particular?" she asked.

"Well . . . yes, Miss Cynthia Poole from Brighton, and her mama, are to attend," he said, his gaze darting across the room.

Lady Dunmore, who would act as Justine's chaperone, and her French companion, Monique, entered. "Mademoiselle de Vauban looks ill. Evidently the sea air is not salubrious to her health," Justine commented.

Hoppy made a *moue*, an oddly feminine pout on his dispassionate face. "No, she has not improved. She's a retiring chit, isn't she?" He stiffened with alertness. "There is Miss Poole now. If you'll excuse me, I'll have to go to her."

Justine noted the young lady right behind Mademoiselle de Vauban. The newcomer had golden ringlets and a shy smile. Hoppy spoke to the lady's mother, then bowed over Miss Poole's hand. She simpered, and Mrs. Poole, a stout matron of middle years, preened at some compliment that

Justine could not hear. She didn't think Hoppy was the kind of young man dedicated to flattering conversation.

Restless, she sipped her ratafia. Charity, dressed in a pale pink silk gown and adorned with pearls around her throat, joined Justine. Excitement seemed to exude from Charity's every pore. "All those I invited have accepted. The evening is bound to be a success."

"You are popular," Justine said, and some of Charity's excitement rubbed off on her. "I'm sure Mademoiselle de Vauban wishes she were in your position."

Charity sighed. "I've tried to befriend her, but she keeps herself to herself. Not one to make friends, alas."

As if she'd heard their conversation, the French miss smiled from across the room and gave a timid wave. Charity fetched her, introducing her to various young gentlemen as she returned to Justine's side.

"Would you like to travel into Brighton to the shops one day?" Justine asked. "I would be glad of your company."

"So would I," Charity said. "There's a French *modiste* who might fashion us new gowns."

Mademoiselle bent her head as she replied, "No, I never go into Brighton on frivolous errands. Certainly not without Lady Dunmore. She needs me constantly."

"I'm sure she would not mind giving you half a day off now and then," Justine said, mentally making a note that she would approach Lady Dunmore with the request herself.

Mademoiselle stiffened. "I have no desire to visit Brighton." She glanced toward Lady Dunmore who was talking to Hoppy. "If you'll excuse me now."

Justine exchanged a curious glance with Charity. They watched the Frenchwoman cross the room in a hurry. Hoppy greeted her warmly as if they'd known each other for a long time. How strange . . .

When the musicians started playing a minuet, Justine found herself claimed by Roger and was immediately pulled into the set.

"Charity is lovely, isn't she?" Roger said dreamily. "I wish she would accept my proposal, but she only laughs, as if my offer of marriage is a laughing matter."

"I doubt I can help you there," Justine said as she followed the figure of the dance.

"You could put in a good word for me," Roger said, his eyes pleading in his flushed face. He stumbled slightly and bumped into another dancing gentleman. "Dashed flatfoot!" he snapped. As the other man glared, Roger added, "Beg pardon."

Justine felt sorry for him. How could he win the lovely and kind Charity's heart if he kept courting strong spirits and making a fool of himself at every gathering.

"I need your advice, Miss Bryerly. What can I do to impress my strong admiration on Charity?"

"If I were you, I would present myself in a sober, responsible fashion. I doubt that Charity looks kindly upon a gentleman who has constant assignments with the brandy bottle."

Roger's face flushed redder. "You don't dilute your words, do you?"

Justine laughed. "*You* asked for my advice—or have you already forgotten? I have to speak the truth."

The dance ended shortly with Roger deep in thought. He led her back to the chaperone and took himself off to another room. Justine danced all evening with various partners, among them Hoppy, who kept staring at her when he didn't stare at Miss Poole. She deftly evaded his advances, but he followed her around and engaged her in conversation at every opportunity.

Around eleven o'clock, half an hour before Henry would come to escort her home, Justine sat down by the chaperone and fanned herself.

Next to her, Lady Dunmore, regal in puce satin and a golden turban, said, "That young man will come to a bad end, mark my words."

"Yes, if he doesn't change, he will," Justine said and wielded her fan faster in front of her hot face. Lady Dunmore studied her with a vulture's interest. "I hear that Nora is prospering. I shall pay her and Baby Diana a visit shortly. Does this mean you will leave the area, Miss Bryerly?"

"I shan't stay here the rest of the year," Justine said, feeling a pang that she would have to leave the happiness of the Allenson household.

"I also heard that Lord Lewington has courted you on and off all spring and now here at Oldhaven."

"You should not listen too closely to gossip," Justine said tartly. "I am in no way attached to the marquess, nor do I encourage his courtship."

"I daresay it is a grand mistake on your part not to set your cap at him," Lady Dunmore said in a judgmental tone of voice. "He is an excellent catch, and mamas all over England have tried to fix his interest on their daughters."

Justine stirred restlessly. "He has no intention of ever marrying, Lady Dunmore. If he had, he would already be married, don't you think?"

Lady Dunmore pursed her lips. "Well, he doesn't shun the local entertainment. There he is now." She pointed with her fan toward the door.

Justine's heart seemed to bounce and lodge in her throat. Her knees weakened, and her breath rasped. She carefully avoided looking toward the door. "I thought he went to London on business."

Lady Dunmore lifted her chin in scorn and turned to speak with a dowager sitting on her other side. Justine eyed the tall French windows and wondered if she could escape through one of them.

From the corner of her eye she noticed Charity and her papa chatting with the marquess. Damien looked very handsome in biscuit pantaloons and a blue coat. His hair gleamed raven black in the candlelight. Justine swallowed hard, commanding her heart to slow down its wild race.

She loved him. She always had loved him, since the first time he laid his lazy gaze on her and grinned. So much had happened since then, and she'd tasted his accomplished flirting, his heady kisses, and his—lies or evasions. She had also glimpsed the pain in his heart and his anger. She was surprised to discover that every part of him, even the darker side, added to her affection. All her pain and frustration fell away for a moment, and that was the exact time he chose to look up, right into her eyes.

The air seemed to crackle across the room, and Justine's heart danced another country reel in her chest.

Then Charity led him across the room. They wove among the waltzing couples and stood before Justine before she'd had time to compose herself.

"Look who I found at the door," Charity said, her eyes teasing Justine.

"I thought you said the marquess would not attend," Justine replied coolly.

Damien's eyes narrowed at the edge of weariness in her voice. "You don't sound very pleased to see me."

Justine remained silent.

"I do love surprises," Charity said as Damien greeted the row of chaperones.

Roger claimed his dance with Charity, and Justine followed the couple with her gaze while feeling like a rabbit trapped by the fox. Warmth suffused her as Damien's gaze found hers.

"Really, why are you sitting here, Justine? You should be dancing every dance." He held out his arm. "May I have the pleasure of this waltz?"

Justine couldn't very well refuse him without seeming rude and unpleasant. Without a word, she stood, folding her fan and letting it fall to the cord around her wrist.

"You look very pensive," he said as he swept her into his arms, his grip on her hand hard and reassuring.

"I can't help but wondering in what way you will provoke me tonight. You always find a way to probe in the most uncomfortable recesses of my mind."

"We have so much unspoken between us, Justine. It's only fair you give us another chance to probe even deeper into each other's secrets."

He danced with long fluid steps, bringing her with him with ease. She let herself be swept up by his exuberance, only seeing his indolent eyes and the small smile tugging at his lips. The other twirling couples became a blur, and she could barely feel her feet touch the floor.

"We do dance so very well together," he said, "just as we do other things in rare unity."

"I cannot think of a single thing that we do together in harmony. We're always at loggerheads, always bickering about something."

His smile widened. "It does add a thrill to life, the clash and thunder of our quarrels."

"I don't make it a habit to quarrel, Damien."

"But admit that you like the spice of adversity, the breath of adventure. Otherwise you would have sent me packing or asked Henry to do it for you."

A reluctance to argue with him further came over her. She kept silent, and his eyebrows rose in question. "Already putting your sword down?"

"I am tired of verbal dueling. Let's just enjoy the dance, and then you can lead me back to the chaperones."

A mask of politeness slowly stiffened on his face. When the dance ended, he did not lead her back to the wall of chaperones; he led her outside.

Couples walked arm in arm along the terrace, so Justine did not fear that he would behave in any way ungentlemanly. Part of her hoped he would.

He guided her along the flagstone surface, his arm hard and reassuring under her hand. A warm humid breeze wafted across the lawn and tickled loose curls at the nape of her neck.

"I sent my mistress packing," he said without preamble, "and I'm not taking another."

Sudden joy flooded her heart. "Why are you telling me this?"

He stopped, pushing her back against the balustrade so that she had to sit down. "You wanted proof that I have changed. Well, that's one tangible change."

"A mistress at the Fisherman's Luck must have caused your aunt great shame." Justine could not find anything more favorable to say.

"She did not know."

"Don't be so sure about that. Gossip is rampant in the

village, and she's bound to hear most of it through her servants."

"I have canceled the lease on my lodgings in St. James's. Next time I rent in London, it will be as a married man. We shall have a respectable family house in Mayfair."

"Was that your business in London?" she asked, thinking of the valise that moldered in her clothespress at Milverly.

"Part of it, yes." He sighed, leaning against one hand propped on the balustrade. "I don't know what I have to do to prove myself to you. Tear my heart out?"

Impulsively she touched his cheek, tracing the hard angle of his jaw. "In many ways, you have already proved yourself, and it gladdens my heart, but I'm afraid there are still secrets between us."

"Secrets? What are you talking about?" His gaze shifted imperceptibly past her shoulder, and she sensed his unease.

"I know there are so many *things* you haven't told me about your life. You were part of the Peninsular campaign, but you never speak of it. And I know you've worked for the Foreign Office, in Wellington's . . . in the . . ." She wished fervently that he would fill in the words "intelligence service," but he said nothing, only clenched his jaw as if her words touched too closely to a hidden part.

"I don't know what you're hinting at, Justine. I did work for Wellington during the Peninsular campaign, and I have kept in contact with him while he's commanding the occupying military forces in France. He has the tremendous and thankless task of helping to restructure the French government and root out any lingering Bonapartist sympathizers among the French people. They have to support the Bourbons fully before Wellington and the allied forces can leave."

She sensed his puzzlement at her interest, but that did not mean he was innocent of selling secrets to the French. "I suppose *you* fully support the Bourbons?"

He looked shocked. "Of course I do! Bonaparte was a madman who would have continued to bring destruction to the Continent. We must make sure that he never returns and that his ideologies are never practiced again."

He spoke with such vehemence, his voice low, but harsh with suppressed fury. "I want to know why you bring politics into our discussion."

"I daresay a courting couple ought to discuss everything."

His face softened, and the hard look left his eyes. "By Jove, *are* we courting?"

She warmed inside, so much so that she longed to reveal her heart in all its glory of emotion and pain. "You have been noted to hound me, and my resistance is weakening."

His face split in a grin. "I'm rendered speechless. Are all my wiles working?"

She clucked her tongue. "There's a long way to go before I can trust you, Damien." She grew quite breathless. "I am, however, *very* fond of you."

"Very . . . ?" he echoed, his face moving dangerously close to her own. His quick breaths wafted over her cheek, tickling her and creating a longing for his kiss.

He loomed closer, his mouth brushing hers, igniting a flare of passion. He stiffened, and she sensed his difficulty controlling himself. Voices and laughter stopped him, however, just as thoroughly as the appearance of a chaperone would have.

"I want to shower your face with kisses, and undress you slowly in the moonlight," he whispered.

Justine shivered with delight, but at the same time felt green and unsophisticated. "I don't know what I would like to do to you, Damien," she said, her voice trembling. "Perhaps seal your lips with glue to spare my ears from listening to your smooth blandishments."

"You would like to hold me and slowly untie my neckcloth and kiss my throat . . . and more."

Justine listened to his daring suggestions and grew hot all over. "Spoken like a true rake." She moved away from him. She noticed vaguely that Monique de Vauban was watching her on the terrace and talking to Hoppy. Through the window, she could see Roger dancing with Charity close by.

"Why are you leaving?" he asked as he caught up with her.

"It is dangerous to my senses to spend time alone with you, Damien."

"I won't force myself upon you."

"I understand, but your forceful presence is enough to set any female's heart fluttering. Your compliments disturb me, as I am sure you have said them before, to different ears."

"That's not true! I don't rehearse my flattery." He sounded frustrated.

"Be that as it may, but how do I know for sure that I'm not only your next conquest to be left bleeding by the side of the road when you tire of me . . . like the last time?"

His face fell, and she could tell he had no explanation that would set her fears to rest. She placed a hand on his arm. "I do want to trust you, but I cannot. Not yet." *Not until the mystery of the valise is solved.* She knew then she had to confide in someone right away. If she didn't, the valise would forever keep them apart.

"But there is hope?" he asked, his eyes intent.

She nodded, unable to swallow the emotion rising in her throat. "Yes."

As they came to the terrace window, she saw Henry speaking with Lady Dunmore, who gestured toward the terrace.

She touched Damien's arm. "I need to warn you about something. Shadwell asked me about you—about your activities at the Crest. He suspects you might be the Fox. I had to tell you."

He drew his breath sharply. "By the devil! What infernal cheek going behind my back and questioning you. I shall—"

"Shh, don't speak so loudly. No need to air this business in public."

His eyes softened. "Thank you for warning me. It means there's a glimmer of trust between us."

Justine thought of the valise and felt rotten for not bringing that up as well. She would have to speak with Henry first, seek his advice.

"Go now. Henry is here to take me home."

Damien hesitated. "My sweetest heart," he said, then kissed her hand and left via the garden.

I don't want anything to stand between us, no secrets, no subterfuge. Justine watched him leave, feeling the loss keenly.

She had to speak before she lost her nerve. As Henry reached her side, she pulled him toward the balustrade. "I have to talk with you right now, Henry. It's very urgent."

Behind Henry stood Shadwell. "Take a walk in the garden, Shadwell," Henry said. He addressed Justine. "I picked him up in Brighton. His horse had gone lame on the way home."

Justine pulled her brother-in-law toward the darkest spot on the terrace. The couples had dispersed, and only occasional steps sounded on the garden path below. She couldn't see anyone among the trees, but tall shrubbery below the railing obscured the paths. Shadwell lingered for a moment below, then disappeared in the shadows. As she gathered her thoughts to speak, Justine was vaguely aware of Roger's and Charity's voices nearby.

"Henry, I pray that I am wrong, but I fear Damien is the person who is selling information to the French." Her voice rose on a note of hysteria, and he placed a calming hand around her shoulders.

"Damien, a French *spy?*" he asked tersely.

"I have a valise at home in my room that might prove his guilt."

Henry held a finger to his lips. "Sssh, not so loud, Justine. We'd better speak of this at home—not here where anyone can overhear us. Let's find Shadwell and be gone."

Justine noticed that Roger and Charity were standing by the window three feet away staring straight at her. She waved and hurried after Henry.

Thirteen

IT TOOK TIME to search for Shadwell in the dark garden, but he could not be found. Justine and Henry happened upon the French companion and Hoppy below the terrace as they stepped down to the brick path. Had they stood behind the shrubbery the whole time overhearing her outburst? Justine wondered as a premonition of disaster skittered along her spine. They nodded politely to Henry as he charged past them. Justine gave them a quick smile and hurried after her brother-in-law.

"Damn that secretary, where is he?" Henry said under his breath, as they sought high and low for Shadwell.

Finally, Charity's father dispatched servants to search for the secretary, but no one discovered his whereabouts.

"Perhaps he walked home. It's not that far," Justine said as Henry paced the hallway at Jasmine Cottage.

"Yes, you may be right." He took her arm. "Let's go back to Milverly."

Justine had thanked her hostess and gathered her belongings. Twenty minutes in the carriage saw them safely home. Henry had not spoken during the entire journey. When they reached Milverly, he sent for Shadwell, then turned to Justine. His face wore creases of worry and lost hope.

"Show me the valise."

They hastened up to Justine's room, where Agnes had left a burning candle. The maid slept on a truckle bed in the dressing room.

"Don't wake her," Henry whispered. "This is just between you and me."

Justine nodded and went in search of the valise in her clothespress. She rummaged among the many hems of her dresses, but her fingers did not encounter the leather hide of the valise.

It simply wasn't there.

She turned to Henry, her worry growing by the minute. "I swear it was here this morning, Henry."

He nodded. "I don't doubt you. Could Agnes have moved it elsewhere?"

Justine shook her head. "No. I told her not to touch it."

"Then someone else removed it. Who else have you told?"

"No one," Justine said, her voice tight with anguish. "But wait! I might still have the money and the paper wrapped around it. I moved them from the back to another spot so as to keep them away from prying eyes."

Henry's jaw dropped. "Your forethought amazes me. Most likely the bundle will free Damien of all suspicion."

"Or condemn him."

Justine found the packet tucked at the very back of the clothespress. It seemed to burn her hand as she realized that her whole future was tied up with this, her future with Damien, if there was to be any.

She handed the bundle to Henry, and in doing so, a burden lifted from her shoulders. Damien's fate did not lie in her hands any longer. It was up to Henry to decide which step to take next, and she knew he would be fair.

She watched as he leafed through the money and studied the coded message. The butler knocked on the door softly, and Henry pushed the packet into his pocket and stepped outside, Justine on his heels.

"Mr. Shadwell is not in his room," the servant said. "He has not returned from Brighton, milord."

Henry nodded curtly and beckoned to Justine to follow

him downstairs. They hurried to the study and closed the door.

"Where could he be?"

"Mayhap he needed to be by himself. I don't worry about him," Henry said.

"Do you know what the code means, Henry?" she asked, her hands trembling with apprehension. *Oh dear God, let Damien be innocent.*

Henry did not respond at once. "I highly doubt Damien is the Fox, but there are things here I don't quite understand." He gave her a thoughtful look. "You might as well know that Damien is working for the Duke of Wellington, and this is obviously part of that business. He promised to help me find the Fox, and there might be some evidence in this packet. I wonder about the money." He set the money down carefully. "How did *you* get involved in the first place, Justine?"

She told him all the details she knew of the valise and how it had mistakenly followed her to Milverly. She also mentioned Damien's appearance at various inns along the way.

Silence hung heavily in the room as she finished. They stared at each other, sharing the rising apprehension.

"He will have a perfectly innocent explanation," Henry said. "The obvious thing to do now is to confront him. I don't want to involve the law at this early juncture. He's a good friend, and I trust him—always have."

Justine nodded, grateful.

"You do care very much about him, don't you, Justine?"

"Yes . . . yes, I do love him—with all my heart, but I dare not reveal the depth of my feelings until this matter is cleared up."

"Very sensible." He glanced at the dark window. "Come, most likely we'll find Damien at home at this late hour."

The carriage was still outside in the drive. Henry assisted Justine inside. In their haste, she'd forgotten her hat and her shawl, but those were the least of her worries.

"I do hope Nora didn't wake up concerned about our whereabouts," she said.

"I left a message. Besides, she knows that I tend to business at odd hours."

Fifteen minutes later they entered the Crest, where a sleepy footman had admitted them. He went in search of the marquess. Roger stepped through the door to one of the salons, and an open window brought a humid warm breeze from the sea. He looked like he'd been running, disheveled and hot. He took an unsteady sidestep and his face split in an inane grin.

"I'll be blowed. You're a sight for sore eyes. Thought I had to drink the last bottle alone. Hoppy's gone off with some boring friends."

"We're not here with the aim to share your brandy, Roger. We're here to see Damien."

The door to the library opened. "And see him you shall," Damien said. His gaze roved from Henry to Justine, evidently sensing the tension. "It is an unusual time for a visit, though."

Roger staggered forward. "I'll have a quiet glass . . . *hic* of brandy with you afterwards, Dam."

"Damien's face tightened in anger. "No you're not. You're going to bed to sleep off the worst." Taking Roger by the collar of his coat, he pushed the young man toward the stairs leading to the private rooms above.

"Damn your hardhanded way, Dam," Roger said, stumbling against the carved oak baluster.

Justine remembered Damien telling her that he once had been like Roger. Relief washed over her as she noticed that Damien was sober and alert. He had truly changed.

They closed the library door, and Justine wished he wouldn't look at her so intently. Could he read her fear, her guilt for not confronting him earlier?

He stood by the desk, his arms crossed over his chest. "What's wrong?"

Henry pulled out the packet. "The thousand pounds and the coded message belong to you, I believe."

Damien's eyes widened as he received the bundle. "*Where* did you find these, Henry? I've searched everywhere."

"In Justine's clothespress."

Damien's gaze flew to her face, and she swallowed with difficulty as anguish clogged her throat. "I . . . I found it in a valise that must belong to you."

"The valise that went missing in Crawley." His lips thinned, and he slapped the packet onto the desk. "Well, really!"

Henry sat down on the edge of the desk, dangling one leg. "A business matter is it?"

Damien heaved a deep audible sigh filled with exasperation. "Yes . . . Roger was supposed to bring the valise back from Crawley, except he got hopelessly brandy-faced and lost the valise."

Silence descended between them as Henry's gaze never left Damien's. Justine felt the rising tension.

"What are you asking me, Henry? Come right out with any accusations you might have."

"I can't decipher the code at this short notice, but I might have to take the paper back with me to London. To the Home Office, and I might have to mention your name."

Damien barked a laugh. "You don't think I'm *the Fox?*" No one replied.

"You can't seriously believe I work for Castlereagh and Wellington besides selling information to the French Bonapartists?"

Henry shook his head and sighed heavily. "No . . . but what am I supposed to believe?"

"The money is not for information sold, but for silks and brandy deliveries to a merchant in Crawley. You might not understand the whole smuggling business, but I have paid part of Father's debts by smuggling foreign goods. I don't keep anything for myself any longer, but I do help the village to survive in these very hard postwar times. I arranged for favorable deals with the merchants."

"I don't blame you for smuggling," Henry said. "In fact, I've suspected you of taking part in it. Oldhaven's men need a leader like you to see them through. My worry is the other part of the packet."

"It is the instructions for my French contact—from Castlereagh's staff. It contains the names of secret Bonapar-

tists in Paris. It is important that they are caught, so that they
don't start another revolution. Europe has been ravished
with war, we don't need another one."

Henry rubbed his round chin in thought. "Hmmm, do you
think the list is a desirable item for the Fox?"

Damien thought for a moment, looking somewhere past
Justine as if she were not in the room. "Yes . . . it's very
possible. If that secret society of Jacobins is shattered, the
Fox's services won't be needed."

Henry stood. "I believe you, Damien. For now anyway,
unless some tangible proof appears that you're indeed the
Fox. I have it on the highest authority that the spy operates
in this area, and that the evidence is mounting even as we
speak. His—or her—identity shall be revealed in short
order. We're very close to discovering the identity of the
traitor."

"I take it you've learned that the spy moves in our
circles," Damien said. "How else would he ferret out the
secret dispatches?"

"Yes . . . unless it's one of the smugglers. Through the
servants they have access to my house, if not the office.
Anyway, all the important papers are locked in a secret
place."

"Secret to you—and—Shadwell," Damien said with a
wry smile.

"I know you don't like that poor fellow very much, but
Shadwell is not a criminal."

"He could have found the valise in my room," Justine
inserted, wanting to catch Damien's attention.

He kept ignoring her, and her alarm rose to unbearable
proportions. Anger seemed to have encased him in glass,
hard and shiny, as if caught in rigid control. He spoke in a
pleasant voice to Henry, and she knew the anger was
directed at her. "What do you know about Shadwell except
that he worked at the War Office and that he's the younger
son of Lord Sweeney?"

"For one thing, he's a Tory and supports the restoration of
the Bourbons wholeheartedly. He has a serious disposition
and is a diligent and hard worker. Most of all, he's loyal."

"You trust him with all the communications from the Home Office?"

Henry nodded. "Yes . . . I might not show him *everything* you understand, but anything that needs my reply, he sees."

"Even secret government business?" Damien's voice was hard, uncompromising.

Henry made a grimace, like a man pushed and held up against a wall. "As I said, he's worthy of confidence. You'll have to trust my judgment on that."

Damien nodded. "Yes, I do. If Shadwell is innocent, who else could be involved? I don't know of anyone who would have access to government bulletins."

"Except you, Damien," Henry said quietly and approached his friend. "I'm sorry I had to bring this up, to voice such a suspicion, but you have to admit the coded message is deuced suspicious."

Damien nodded curtly and accepted Henry's outstretched hand. "We'll get to the bottom of this somehow. All we know is that someone has access to the bulletins that are passed along to our army in France."

"Yes. Henry, if you don't mind, I would like to speak with Miss Bryerly alone for a few minutes."

Henry glanced speculatively at Justine. "Do you want to speak to him unchaperoned, Justine?" Henry's mouth curved in a small smile. "I expect he won't act like a beast."

Justine nodded, her whole body trembling with the ordeal to come.

"I shall wait for you in the hallway." He addressed Damien. "Mind you, only five minutes."

He closed the door behind him.

"So, *you* suspected all along I was the Fox, eh?" Damien asked in a hard voice.

Justine leaned against the back of a chair to keep herself safely anchored to the props of ordinary life. "I didn't know what to believe. I still don't—not really, but I had to show my find to someone whom I trusted."

His eyes blazed, and his voice held an edge of frost. "Why didn't you confront me directly, Justine? Why did you hold back, never telling anyone about the valise?" He slammed his fist against the top of the desk. "How could you spend so much time with me, listening to my lovesick confessions while keeping the valise a secret?"

"I wasn't strong enough to face the possibility that you might be the Fox, but now I have to know, to find out if we have a future together." She held out her hand in a pleading gesture. "I wanted so much to reveal my secret, especially after tonight at the dance, but I could not. My secret was a great responsibility to—England, not just to the people around me."

"He quieted down somewhat, his sighs deep and filled with frustration. "Oh, Justine, why didn't you come to me those many weeks ago when you learned the valise belonged to me? Why didn't you trust me?"

"I just couldn't. I wanted no more than to stay out of your life. Bringing the valise to your attention would only have dredged up the past, a past I wanted to forget, not relive. I couldn't stand more humiliation like the one you brought me in London."

He gave her a sharp glance. "Yes. I acted irresponsibly and irrationally. There's no excuse for it, but my separation from you showed me how much I needed you, how much I've come to care about you." He gave her another intent stare. *"Justine—"*

A knock sounded on the door and Henry put his head into the room. "Everything explained? Your five minutes have passed."

Justine gave Damien a pleading glance. "Please forgive me for keeping this from you. I worried about it constantly but only now dared to confront my suspicions."

Damien's lips tightened, and Justine could sense his anger with her. "Well, I daresay we shall find the real culprit soon. Meanwhile, I will have to work on uncovering his or her identity if I'm ever to have a future with you."

"Fair enough," Henry said as he took Justine's hand and pulled her toward the door. "We shan't sit idle at Milverly. If we put our heads together we might conceive a clever trap."

"Yes . . . I'll ride over to lend my support. I know I won't sleep until the traitor is caught."

Justine threw a glance over her shoulder at her beloved. His hand crumpled the bank notes, and a look of despair filled his face.

The Fox was still standing between them.

Fourteen

"Oh, Henry, what are we going to do?" Justine asked as they rode home. "I can't bear the thought that there's the slightest possibility that Damien might be guilty of treason." She shook her head. "I *won't* believe it. I can't."

Henry's shoulders slumped as if weighed down with too heavy a burden. "I can't either." He slapped his knee. "We shall contrive a trap somehow, a way to lure the real spy into our net. Since you're already involved, you will have to help me find a solution."

"Yes . . . when he or she discovers that the coded message is no longer in the valise, the spy will perhaps return to investigate my room further."

"That is an excellent point."

Justine sighed, thinking of the people she'd met at various houses in the area. "Henry, if you're sure that Shadwell and Damien are innocent, who do you think is the real spy?"

"Difficult to say. There are many soldiers from the wars, out of the army and desperate to gain an income. Times are very hard for the less fortunate."

"I don't know any soldiers or former soldiers. Could the spy be Mademoiselle de Vauban or one of the young gentlemen who court Charity? Both Roger and Hoppy seem reckless enough for any lark."

"It would be terrible for their families to learn that one of their own is capable of treason." His voice sank as if tired, but she knew he commiserated with Damien.

"Damien would be devastated to find out that Roger is the Fox," she said, as anguish rolled in her stomach.

"I would not be surprised if Roger is involved. He's a wild young man and often flaunts his lack of respect for authority." Henry sighed and shook his head as though unable to believe the ways of the world. "A lack of authority is rather common among the reckless town bloods. I recall certain wild events of my younger years. We used to go into the streets and overturn the huts of the Charlies—the watchmen—while they stood inside."

Justine smiled. "'Tis difficult to picture you involved in such a disrespectful event, Henry. You've always seemed so steady and responsible."

"A thoroughly dull dog, eh?"

"I didn't mean that, but surely Damien led you into these pranks."

Henry did not confirm that suspicion. "I have known Damien a long time. He is—was—capable of a lot of pranks, but not treason."

That assurance will have to be enough, Justine thought. She would have to remember that over and over while they searched for the real traitor.

The carriage arrived at Milverly just as a storm broke loose, pouring sheets of cold rain over the already muddy yard. One of the footmen came out carrying umbrellas.

"I shall endeavor to find out more about Mademoiselle de Vauban tomorrow. At least it is a start!" Justine shouted over the rustle of the rain.

Justine sought out Charity the next morning. Mist filled every hollow, and water dripped from every branch. The grass lay sodden, flattened by rain that it could no longer tolerate.

The crops will fail and people will starve, Justine thought with an uneasy shiver. *The English will suffer more hardships even if the wars are over.*

Shaking off her morose thoughts, she alighted from her horse at Charity's front door. Charity received her in the parlor right by the entrance.

"You look glum," she said after hugging Justine. "Is it due to this dismal rain or is your heart at peril of breaking once more?"

Justine grimaced and gave her friend a penetrating look. "Breaking? Utter nonsense. I only wanted to thank you for an entertaining evening—even if the Marquess of Lewington arrived despite your assurance that he would not attend."

"Fie, Justine. I did not know he would be back from London in time for my dance. I had to invite him, you understand. I'm certain he only came to see you." She sat down, settling the folds of her sprigged muslin gown. Blue ribbons bounced in her blond curls, and she fiddled with a lace fichu at her neck. She patted the sofa. "Sit down, Justine, and tell me what happened. You disappeared rather abruptly with Lord Allenson, but Damien left rather more quickly. Your comings and goings made my head spin."

She looked closely at Justine. "You do look peaked, Justine. Is there something the matter?"

Justine did not want to divulge information about the spy to Charity. The fewer who knew, the better.

"I'm only curious about Graham Hopper. I danced with him last night, and he seems very interested in me."

Charity flung out her arms and laughed. "Is that all? I thought by your expression that something dreadful had happened at Milverly."

Justine shook her head. "No, not at all. Everyone is fine, but tell me, what do you know about Hoppy? I heard a rumor from the servants that he meets someone in Brighton. A young lady, I wonder? Miss Poole, who was at your gathering? He flirted with her as well."

"That could be true. I don't know anything about Mr. Hopper. He's charming in a rather shallow way, keeps all of his opinions to himself. Roger, however, bares his heart at every opportunity." Charity made a grimace. "'Tis the bottle that talks, not he. Roger is tedious when he's in his cups."

"Which he is more often than not."

Charity made another grimace. "Yes—unfortunately. He would be more attractive without his frequent meetings with the bottle."

"I think he's rather lonely."

"And he feels worthless beside his older brother, who always berates Roger for his behavior," Charity said pertly. "As if Damien was not wild in his younger days, just like Roger."

Silence hung between them for a while, and Justine was surprised to discover that she had to defend Damien. She saw his motive clearly. "Damien worries about Roger; he would like to see Roger happy, see him safely on a path with some meaning."

As she spoke the words, Justine knew they were true. She had not thought of Damien in those terms, as those of a concerned man who understood Roger's dilemma.

"Papa will never approve of Roger's suit if he continues to come here while castaway." Charity sighed. She pounded her fist against the velvet cushion in her lap. "I don't know what will change Roger's behavior. Admonitions run off him like water off a duck's back."

"He will have to come to the crossroads alone, make a decision to change. At least he's not courting someone else, Charity. He has eyes for no one but you."

Charity smiled. "That's true. He does not dash off to Brighton to meet his paramour. By the way, speaking of meeting someone clandestinely, I saw the mousy Monique in Brighton. She was having tea with a gentleman stranger at the local inn."

"She said she never traveled to Brighton." Justine's spine tingled as if she'd stumbled on a surprise that had the power to change the course of everything. "Are you sure it was a stranger? Not one of Oldhaven's gentlemen?"

"I don't know; I couldn't see him very well, only the back of him, but I'd say I never saw the gentleman before. He had a foreign air, dark hair, and a sun-bronzed complexion. Mayhap he was a Frenchman, someone she used to know."

"Still, she was very young when she came to live with Lady Dunmore. What kind of ties could she have with

France? Her infamous brother? How and when would she make friends with a Frenchman? It was a miracle that Lady Dunmore let her go off to Brighton alone."

"Perhaps Lady Dunmore spent the morning fitting dresses at the *modiste's,* and Monique took a walk without her employer knowing about it."

"I'm so curious about her," Justine said in an exaggerated voice. "She speaks very little about herself, and I would like to know more about her strange past."

Charity shuddered. "I'm not sure *I* want to know more about the past of France. It must have been horrible to live through the Terror. I would have been broken to lose my entire family and my home."

Justine nodded in agreement. Filled with nervous energy, she got up. "I'd better go back to Milverly before Nora sends out someone to look for me."

Charity accompanied her to the door. "I'm sorry you had to meet Damien last night, but you're bound to meet occasionally since you live in the same village." She hugged Justine. "Try to talk some sense into Roger for me."

"I will try, but I'm afraid my advice will fall to deaf ears."

Roger was at that moment staring morosely out to sea from the window. A special messenger rode hard up the drive. Foam flecked along the flanks of the post horse, and Roger wondered what business could be so urgent. If only Damien would share more of his affairs, but he only looked askance when Roger offered to help with the estate matters. Roger, you're useless, Damien's eyes seemed to say every time. I can't trust you with the smallest responsibilities. Faugh!

Damien could trust me, Roger thought, but Damien never tried, not after the last fiasco in Crawley.

Pain pounded at his temples as he reached for the fresh decanter of brandy. One, or two glasses at the most, would draw a pleasant veil over the problems always nagging at his mind. They would nag him to death one day, if the feeling of uselessness didn't urge him to drive his team over the steep cliffs along the sea. With a trembling hand, he reached for the decanter and gripped his glass as if it were the only solid form to hold on to. . . .

Damien received the packet from Struthers, who had dealt with the messenger. This must be the report from the old Bow Street Runner he'd hired to find out more about Hoppy's past. His heart began to beat faster as if he sensed that Hoppy's past would reveal a clue to the Fox—or even the spy himself.

Damien sat down behind his desk and cracked the red seal of wax. The packet held several stiff papers, one a letter, another dates dutifully copied from ledgers and registers. First he read the letter:

My Lord Marquess,

I have dealt most satisfactory with the matter you hired me to do, but I am humbled to say that there is not much to report on your young Mr. Hopper. He hails from Faringdon, Oxfordshire, as my carefully written copy of his birth records will attest. He's the son of an impoverished country gentleman, whose oldest brother was a baronet by appointment.

Graham Hopper in due time received a small inheritance from his grandmother, which allowed him to enter university at Oxford, where he, by the way, no longer resides. An indifferent student, he spent most of his time gambling, that way paying for his upkeep and eventual debts. Among his former cronies, he has rather the reputation of a card shark, and a man who likes his claret. There was some sort of scandal in the family, the whisper of the older brother being tried by court-marshal after deserting the army in the Peninsula. The locals knew little about the matter, and I shall endeavor to discover more at the War Office in London. Expect a later communication from me.

I have the honor to be,
Your obedient servant,
Thaddeus Sykes.

Damien dropped the letter onto the desk and stared at nothing. Hoppy had been telling the truth about his family, except for the part about the scandal. He had a fondness for the bottle, and that's how he'd made friends with Roger. Gambling was another vice that had brought them together. Hoppy had eagerly accepted the invitation to stay the summer at Ardmore Crest in exchange for companionship. If not an outright mushroom, Hoppy was an opportunist who knew how to find someone to foot his bills.

Damien felt an urge to slam his fist into the desk, but here was nothing that he didn't already know about Hoppy. He had accepted the young man's presence because of Roger, maybe hoping beyond hope that Hoppy would somehow help Roger back onto the narrow path that would save his life.

Damien rested his head in his hands and muttered, "God, what am I to do? I can't throw Hoppy out until I know for sure he's innocent of spying, but how can I face him without punching his smug face?"

He heaved a tired sigh; there was nothing he could do at the moment. He hadn't really gotten any closer to the truth. Hoppy knew about the smuggling activities and who knows what else? Had he been with Roger when Roger contacted the merchant in Crawley about the valise? He could not bear to think the thought to the end as it made him feel as though he'd failed Wellington and his country.

It wasn't just the disaster of the valise. He'd thought he could count on Roger's support. Therein lay the failure. He was slowly losing his grip, his concentration, the most important trait of an international spy.

He could only hope that the Fox had lost his special "touch" as well or Damien might be the man who would find himself before the magistrates.

Fifteen

"ANYONE COULD HAVE heard us speak about the valise," Henry said to Justine on the following day. "The people strolled in the garden below—including Mr. Hopper and the Frenchwoman, and you spoke rather loudly."

Justine nodded. "It was thoughtless, but I was very worried, and I still am. I'm sorry if I've made it more difficult for you."

Henry shook his head and pulled his hands through his thinning hair. "I discovered that Shadwell spent the night indisposed in his room. He got violently sick to his stomach as he left us at Jasmine Cottage. Too embarrassed to see me—or so he says—he walked straight home where he went to bed. He's still there."

Justine perched on the Chippendale chair by the open terrace door. The breeze played with the chintz curtains and ruffled the hem of her light blue muslin gown. "We know that Mademoiselle de Vauban and perhaps Shadwell and Hoppy Hopper, could have overheard us. Then there was Roger Trowbridge and my friend Charity chatting by the window, though I doubt she had anything to do with the valise. Someone left the gathering and went to Milverly ahead of us to fetch the valise."

A knock sounded on the door as Henry was about to

speak. Damien entered, his face haggard, and his eyes surrounded with dark rings of fatigue.

"Anything new since last?" Henry asked and got up from his desk.

"Not really. I received a report about Hoppy's past. He is who he says, but I'm waiting to hear more about a scandal in the family. Perhaps that will tie him to the Fox."

"I had a bulletin from one of my associates in London," Henry said. "He suggested that Shadwell has Jacobin leanings. But damn it all, I can't believe it! Sorry about my language." He threw his arms in the air. "I trust the fellow!"

"Where did your friend get the idea Shadwell is a Jacobin?"

"They attended some clandestine meetings together, but that doesn't mean Shadwell— He could have attended to discover the identity of the others."

"Have you confronted Shadwell about this?" Damien asked, then flung himself into a chair. He sprawled out his legs and glanced at Justine fixedly. He exuded restrained anger.

Her heart raced at his penetrating stare, but this was not the time to think romantic thoughts. She hoped she would have the chance to tell him she supported him, loved him enough to stand by him, no matter what.

"No, by God, that would tip my hand, wouldn't it?"

Damien nodded. "We'll have to ferret deeper. I'm about to meet with my French contact soon, and he might bring some information from the other side of the Channel."

"According to the official reports, the Duke of Richelieu has made excellent progress in clearing the city of Paris of the Bonapartist fanatics," Henry said. "He wants to get rid of the occupying armies so that the French can get back to the business of putting their country back together. The allied forces will only leave when the Bourbon rule has been firmly reestablished."

Justine sensed the heavy burden of responsibility Henry carried. He was not only the affable and loving Lord Allenson; he worked tirelessly for his country. England desperately needed people like him to get back onto even keel again.

"We can only wait," she said to no one but herself.

"At least until we know more about the people possibly involved."

"We could force his—or her—hand," Damien said, running his knuckles along the polished wood of the armrest. "Contrive a gathering where we could let some information seep out to see if the spy is willing to take risks."

"Extremely dangerous," Henry said and shuffled some papers into untidy stacks.

"We could have a dinner party here celebrating the birth of Baby Diana," Justine suggested. "Then hint at the table that important information is passing through this house on its way to France."

"It is a far-fetched possibility that the spy would fall for that, but better than nothing," Damien said and flashed a dazzling smile at her.

Her knees softened, but she did not want to acknowledge the weakness. Because she was sitting down, he wouldn't notice that, she thought, but he might notice the heat in her cheeks. A blush that says everything.

Henry sat down heavily. "Very well. It is as good a plan as any. Confound it, we have to bring the villain to our very own doorstep to catch him!"

"He might already reside here if his name is Shadwell," Justine said.

"You're right," Damien said, "but we don't know that. To protect the guests we'll bring in some of the smugglers— armed—to guard the grounds. No one needs to know about our plans. For most guests, it's only a regular dinner party."

"I dislike keeping Nora out of the picture."

"She will worry too much and ruin everything," Justine said quickly.

Henry's mouth curved upward at the corners. "And what about you, Justine? Are you going to ruin our plans with a fit of the vapors?"

"Don't be foolish, Henry! I never succumb to the vapors."

Henry laughed, but his mirth was not long-lived. "I wish to God we knew who the Fox is!"

Damien left shortly after their discussion, and Justine accompanied him to the door. They stared long and hard at each other. Finally, longing to kiss away the lines between his eyes, she touched his face. "Damien, I want you to know I believe you're innocent. But even if you weren't, I would still stand by you." Her voice petered out as she dared to bare her innermost feelings.

He grinned and caught her in his arms, crushing her in an embrace. "Thank you, my sweetest heart!" He slowly pulled away. His gaze searched her face, and she could see the faint shadow in his eyes. He continued. "I wish, however, that you had not kept the secret of the valise from me. I cannot but feel it was deceptive."

She nodded. "It was wrong. I acted cowardly."

Silence stretched between them for the longest moment. "We'll talk later. I have to leave now."

Wondering if he would fully forgive her for her mistrust and her secrets, she watched his back as he hurriedly left. She wandered aimlessly around the house. Diana had taken Eddie to visit one of her old cronies outside Brighton, so she could not ease the tedium of the day. Afternoon dragged on into early evening.

Nora rested, and so did the new baby. The air seemed too still, as if breathlessly waiting for chaos to break loose, Justine thought as she looked out the window in the hallway. At least the rain had temporarily let up.

She noticed a rider coming up the curving drive, a female indicated by the long skirt spread over the horse's flank. Soon she recognized the familiar figure of her friend Charity. Her mood brightened at the prospect of a cozy chat.

The footman opened the door, and a stable lad ran up to help Charity down from her mount. "Wait here," she said to the boy.

"Am I happy to see you!" Justine said as she greeted her friend.

"I'm bored to flinders with all this rain," Charity cried

and pulled her gloves off impatiently. "When it finally let up a bit, I decided to pay you a visit."

Justine stared at Charity's golden brown velvet habit, trimmed with narrow brown braid, and felt an urge for some exercise. "I'm terribly bored staying inside all day. Wait until I've changed, and we'll take a ride together."

Charity adjusted the feather curling from the hat brim. "A splendid idea. I've been closed in the house all day."

They set out as the shadows lengthened.

"You came alone?" Justine asked.

"No, one of the grooms accompanied me, but his horse went lame. I sent him back home. Let's not bring anyone. They will only slow us down."

"Yes. But one of the Allenson grooms will take you back home later."

"Pooh! I'm not afraid to ride alone. Jasmine Cottage is only minutes away," Charity said as they turned their horses onto the road. "Come, let's gallop. I can't wait to feel that I'm *alive.*" Charity gave an unladylike shout and set her heels into the side of her mare.

Justine gave an answering loud cry, just as eager to feel the wind cooling her face after the still, heavy afternoon. She longed to forget her nagging worries, but the puzzle of the Fox's identity seemed unsolvable.

Charity's horse kicked up clods of mud, and her skirt flared with each movement.

"Be careful," Justine shouted—to deaf ears. She knew about the many pot holes, with which Charity might not be familiar.

Justine slowed down as her breath grew labored with the exertion. Heat closed around her like a damp blanket. Perspiration started to trickle down the sides of her face. "Wait! Slow down, Charity."

Not hearing the warning, Charity disappeared around a bend in the road.

Suddenly, a cry split the humid air, and Justine's breath stopped in her throat. She urged Columbine to a faster trot, and soon found Charity on the ground, her habit torn and muddy, her horse gone.

"Charity? What happened?" Justine slipped off her horse and kneeled beside her friend.

Charity sat up, her eyes unfocused. She dragged her muddy hand across her brow.

"Are you in pain?"

Charity shook her head. "No . . . only dazed. That dashed horse veered aside for something, and I lost my balance and fell off."

Justine slid her arm around Charity's shoulders. "Are you sure you don't have any broken bones?"

"Yes, yes, I'm fine." Charity looked back at the road. "There's a big hole. My horse must have avoided it." She struggled to her feet, swaying. "Oh dear, look at me! Such a bedraggled state. I look like a street urchin."

"At least you didn't break your neck." Justine stared at the empty road. "Should I try to find your horse?"

"No . . . she's gone back home. She always does when she throws the rider. Father or one of the grooms will come looking for me."

"We can ride together on Columbine." Justine didn't know how she would get back into the sidesaddle without assistance. "I'll help you up and lead the horse home. It's not that far."

Charity protested. "It would be faster if you rode over to Milverly or Jasmine Cottage for another horse."

They tried to get onto Columbine, one after the other, by stepping on the largest rock next to the road, but the heavy riding skirt hampered the movements of the one trying to climb up behind the saddle. Failing, they stared at each other and grimaced.

"I'll wait here, Justine. There's nothing else for it." Still standing on the rock, she assisted Justine into the saddle and slapped the mare on the rump.

"I'll hurry back. Don't worry, Charity." Feeling torn at leaving her friend by the side of the road, she hurried back toward Milverly. Darkness had almost fallen by now, and it would be utterly dark by the time she returned with another horse.

"Dash it all," Justine said to herself and urged Columbine

to a faster speed. Raindrops started falling, big, heavy drops that spread over everything in a trice.

Half a mile down the lane, she came upon a curricle and pair. The driver wore the coat collar up against the pouring rain and a beaver hat pulled low over the eyes. The equipage seemed to weave from one side of the lane to the other, and Justine pulled hard on the reins to prevent a collision with the vehicle.

"Blast and damn!" the driver swore, and Justine recognized Roger Trowbridge's voice. He came to a halt beside her, one of the wheels almost brushing the mare's front leg.

"Mr. Trowbridge, I'm relieved to see you. Mayhap you can help us." Just as the words were out of her mouth, she doubted that involving him would help their cause. Clearly the young man was deeply inebriated and could not be trusted with Charity's safety. But the words had already slipped out.

"What's the m-matter, Miss Bryerly?" he asked, and tried to hide a belch behind his hand.

The rain became a downpour, and already sodden, Justine realized she really needed his help.

"Miss Thornton was thrown off her horse down the road. She's waiting for me to fetch another horse. Perhaps you could—"

"Dashed unpleasant for her," he cried out, but he looked rather delighted with the situation. This would give him another opportunity to court Charity without the supervision of her chaperone, Justine thought.

"We can't let her get soaked to the bone. I shall drive her home myself. Show me the way." He pulled back onto the lane, and Justine rode a bit in front of the carriage while keeping her head down to protect her eyes from the stinging rain.

Charity's forlorn face lit up with relief as they arrived. "You've returned already. Thank heaven for that."

Roger staggered out of the carriage, and Justine watched him with some misgiving. "Are you willing to ride home with him?" Justine cried over the pelting rain. "I'll come along as well."

Charity nodded, her wet ostrich plume slapping against her cheek. "Yes . . . anything to get out of this dreadful weather."

"You might catch inflammation of the lungs," Roger said, trying to look serious but failing miserably. He rather liked his role as rescuer of damsels in distress, Justine thought.

They set off, and soon they could hear the crashing of the sea waves not far away. The lane went into a series of curves, and Roger slowed his reckless pace. Justine could breathe slightly more easily as she followed behind on Columbine, whose hide was steaming by now.

She could barely see the road as darkness compressed around them. The curricle weaved precariously among the deeper puddles.

Before Justine had the chance to shout a warning, Roger took one turn too wide, and two of the wheels ended up in the deep ditch. The light carriage overturned, throwing Charity outside and pinning her. Justine screamed, and Roger lurched out the other side, tumbling headlong into the mud.

The pair of horses were down on their knees, the skewed shackles chafing against their flanks as they struggled to get up.

"Help!" cried Charity, and Justine slid from her saddle. Relieved to hear that Charity was still alive, she hurried to her friend and started pulling at the carriage, but without much success.

Roger swayed beside her, his breath reeking of brandy. "Look what you did!" Justine snapped. "It's possible you've broken Charity's legs with your careless driving."

Roger hung his head, his hands flailing as he fought to control the frightened horses. They stood, pulling the curricle forward. The side lying on top of Charity scraped over the ground. "Whoa!"

"Dear God, can you feel your legs, Charity?" Justine asked and sank down beside her friend still pinned by the vehicle.

"I'm fortunate. It seems like I'm lying in a hollow of sorts," Charity said breathlessly. Justine touched the pale face she could barely see, and she felt the trembling going through Charity.

"We have to get you away from here posthaste."

"At least I'm partly protected from the rain," Charity said in a show of flippancy. Her voice sounded thin and woebegone.

Roger and Justine tried to lift the curricle, but the wheels had mired in mud that kept sucking them down. Justine worked hard until her arms ached, then grew stiff and numb. "We can't shift it," she said and slumped onto her backside in the grass.

"Damien was leaving the tavern just as I was pulled out of the yard," Roger said. "He should be coming along soon."

"He could have taken another road," Justine said.

Roger shook his head. "This is the fastest road to the Crest. I'll wager he doesn't want to be outdoors on a night like this. If he . . . *hic* . . . doesn't arrive soon, I'll fetch him."

True enough, Damien's horse trotted along the road within minutes. They heard him before they saw his dark outline.

"Damien!" Roger shouted. "A slight accident here."

Damien halted his horse abruptly, staring down at them in the gloom. The dense curtain of rain seemed to sway over the road.

Damien snorted with disgust. "Too jug-bitten to see the road clearly? Who are your companions, Roger?"

"It's me and Miss Thornton," Justine said, then stood. "Charity is pinned under the carriage, but fortunately unhurt so far. Can you help us please?"

"By thunder! You are jesting, aren't you?" He got off his horse instantly.

"I'm afraid not." As they struggled to right the curricle and put it back on its wheels, she described the events that had gone before the accident.

She wiped her brow, her hand smearing mud all over. "Oh, no!" she said. "I must look a fright."

"No one can see you," Damien said. He put a steadying

hand on her elbow. "Roger was too inebriated to drive; surely you must have seen that?"

Justine glared at his face above her, though she couldn't see him clearly. "I made a mistake, yes, but I had no choice if I wanted to rescue Charity before total darkness. I had no idea our outing would end up like this." She pushed aside the drooping plumes on her riding hat, but they lashed back. Angry with herself, and with Damien's remarks, she tore the hat off and hurled it into the thicket by the road.

"Good riddance!" She glowered at Damien, but he only laughed. "Well, are you going to just stand there?"

Roger had helped Charity to her feet, and though confessing to feeling shaken, she was whole. Roger led her onto the lane.

"Don't create any more damage than you already have!" Damien snarled to Roger. He pulled the young man away from Charity, and Justine lent a supportive arm to her friend.

"How could you be so cork-brained as to drive your curricle into the ditch?" Damien yelled, shaking his younger brother. "You could have killed a young lady, all owing to your love affair with the brandy bottle."

Justine and Charity listened to his anger and his frustration pouring forth. "Could you have lived with that, Roger? Eh? Could you have lived knowing you'd killed a young innocent lady?"

Roger hung his head; his entire frame drooped. "No . . . n-no! I could not have lived with that. But it didn't happen."

Damien punched Roger's face without another word. Roger crumpled to the ground, moaning. Damien pulled him up by his lapels, and Roger tried halfheartedly to fight, throwing lame punches at any part of Damien's body he could reach.

Damien ended up punching Roger until he staggered over to the curricle and hung over its side, sobbing. Damien dropped his arms to his sides, and a deep sigh went through him, loud enough to penetrate the heavy rustling of the rain. He went to sooth the carriage horses and adjust their harnesses.

Roger muttered something and staggered over the road. "I'm sorry," he said, sobbing. "So s-sorry." He fell to his knees and was sick.

Embarrassed to be a witness, Justine stood as if frozen watching the drama of the brothers' struggle. Damien seemed to be fighting with some inner argument as he leaned his head against the neck of one horse.

The scene froze and no one moved for a long time. Then Roger got up and started walking away.

"Aren't you going to say something?" Charity asked Damien in a trembling voice. "He was contrite; he apologized."

"It is not enough! He could have killed you with his carelessness," Damien said angrily. "Let him ponder that for a day or two."

Justine felt he was right, but her heart still went out to the stoop-shouldered figure hurrying down the muddy lane, his gait uneven and stumbling. Roger could never do anything right, no matter how hard he tried.

"I'll drive you home, Miss Thornton. There's nothing wrong with the curricle, only mud that might ruin your habit."

"It can't get more muddy than it already is," Charity said, trying to brush the gluey substance from her skirt.

Damien tied his horse to the back and assisted Justine into her saddle. His hand lingered on hers. "I wish you had not witnessed the fight with my brother, but I knew it would happen sooner or later."

Justine nodded. "I shudder to think about what might have happened."

Damien squeezed her hand. "I'm sorry about this debacle."

Longing sank through Justine at his touch, but she felt farther away from him than she had in a long time—all because of the unanswered questions between them. "I'm grateful that you came along."

"I'll take you both to Jasmine Cottage and have a message sent over to Milverly that you're safe."

"Yes, thank you, I would like to stay with Charity until she has recovered."

They set off in the dark and reached Jasmine Cottage without another mishap. Damien explained everything to Charity's father, not holding back the shortcomings of his brother.

"I hope that young simpleton has learned a lesson from this or I might feel inclined to teach him another one," Mr. Thornton said darkly. He put Charity into the care of her maid, and Justine followed her upstairs—even though she longed to speak with Damien, who seemed distracted.

She heard him take a hurried farewell of Mr. Thornton and leave.

Damien drove back to Ardmore Crest with his horse tied to the back of the curricle. He wondered if he would find Roger slumped in some ditch, but there was no sign of his brother. Heavyhearted, Damien entered the house after taking the equipage down to the stables. There was no sign of Roger in the study, only Hoppy snoozing by the fire.

Damien had no desire to speak with the guest. Tired and wet, he went upstairs to change clothes. In an hour he would rendezvous with the Frenchmen in the cove below the estate.

The excisemen had been patrolling more frequently, and reinforcement had been sent to the area. Damien feared that sooner or later the smugglers would be caught red-handed.

He would tell Jacques to find another route for future information.

At eleven o'clock he crept down to the cove, all the while on the lookout for the militia. Nothing stirred except the restless sea. There were no signs of the smugglers, only Ben Bryman, waiting behind the rocky outcrops.

"They are there, milord. Just sent the signal," Ben whispered. "They're heading in. I'll go fetch the other men hiding in the thicket at the lower end of the Crest."

"This should be the last run for a while," Damien whispered back. "The situation is too dangerous."

"Aye. We've been lucky so far, but we won't take any risks we can't handle."

Ben disappeared, soundless like a shadow, and Damien kept staring at the pitch black sea. His oilcloth cloak hampered his movements but protected him from the incessant rain. The smugglers arrived, one by one, and waited for the dinghies to arrive. Two of them materialized from the darkness, their prows scraping the shale as they landed.

Jacques jumped out of the first boat. "Monsieur le Marquis?" he whispered, and Damien took the Frenchman's shoulder and hauled him aside.

"Jacques, my clever friend, I'm here. Have you discovered anything about the Fox?"

Jacques nodded eagerly. "*Mais oui,* the Fox was an English gentleman. The Fox is dead. He died in Paris, not six months ago."

Damien frowned, his head starting to ache. "But there's still someone sending important government secrets to the wrong hands in Paris."

Jacques gave a Gallic shrug. "I'm trying to locate the source. *Sacré bleu,* I hate the Jacobins!" He spat on the ground to accentuate his contempt.

Damien felt pinned to a wall, helpless and frustrated. "You can't come back here for some time because of the danger. I'll have to discover the imposter's identity on this side. I think we're close to solving the riddle, but not close enough. He might slip through our fingers."

They watched in silence as the smugglers hurried through the chore of unloading the contraband. Without a sound, they disappeared into the night. It was the fastest transfer Damien had witnessed.

He slapped Jacques's back. "Take care my friend. We have gone through some difficult times since the Peninsular War, but it'll soon be over."

Jacques grinned and jumped into the last dinghy. "Walk with *le Bon Dieu,* Monsieur."

Sixteen

JUSTINE STRAIGHTENED THE bodice of her pale green silk gown and adjusted the lace edging the neckline. She clasped a strand of pearls around her neck and watched as Agnes pinned a bunch of yellow silk roses to her hair. A touch of rouge on her pale cheeks and a touch of powder applied with a hare's foot on her neck and forehead completed her toilette.

Her heart hammered uncomfortably, and her knees seemed to have lost their substance as she walked downstairs. Tonight those in on the plan would make a grand—desperate—effort to discover the identity of the Fox.

Henry had laid out the plan, and Nora had blissfully arranged the dinner party. She knew nothing about the Fox; she thought the dinner party was in celebration of her new baby daughter. It was, and Henry showed nothing of his inner turmoil as he greeted Justine in the hallway.

"You look adorable as usual, Sister," he said and beamed.

How can he look so unperturbed? Diplomatic skills, no doubt, Justine thought.

She admired his flawless neckcloth and his well-fitting coat. "For a politician, you look handsome," she said, trying to add a lighthearted tone.

"Politicians are supposed to look dapper," he said with a

wink. They strolled together into the dining room where Nora was discussing details with the butler. She wore a deep blue gown with gold bands around the hem and the sleeves. Gold glittered in her ears and around her neck.

She gave Justine a penetrating glance. "You look Friday-faced and tired, Justine. Is your stay here very taxing?"

"No . . . not at all! I've enjoyed my stay here, Nora. I slept badly last night, that's all." *Excuses,* she added silently. She would not get any real rest until the Fox was caught and all doubt removed from Damien.

Eddie came running down the stairs, his harried nurse in hot pursuit. "You said I could come down for an ice before going to bed, Mama!" he yelled.

"Yes, you may have an ice or the guests will eat them all," Nora said with a laugh. "Come along, you uncouth boy."

Eddie leered at his nurse. "I told you so!"

Justine noted his bulging pockets and wondered with a shudder what they concealed. She didn't really want to know, but she rubbed his silky head and winked at him. He grinned and scampered off to the kitchen.

The guests soon arrived, a short line of carriages that delivered Lady Dunmore and Monique de Vauban, Mr. Thornton and Charity, Miss Clara Trowbridge, Damien, Hoppy Hopper and Roger from the Crest, and Lady Stanton with her daughter in tow.

Shadwell joined the group unobtrusively. He looked slightly uneasy at mingling with the guests of his employer. Justine knew Henry had invited him to dinner for one reason, one reason only. To discover if he was the Fox.

Damien came toward her. Justine's throat tightened as she admired him dressed in black evening clothes and a pristine neckcloth tied expertly in a Mathematical knot.

Lady Dunmore sailed in like a barge, her mousy companion scurrying in her wake. "This house is lovely," Lady Dunmore exclaimed. "So polished, and so many winking candles. 'Tis hard to find good help who are willing to care for a grand house." She gave Monique a dark look, and the Frenchwoman shrunk visibly.

Nora had returned in time to greet the guests. "The

servants who are happy don't mind hard work," she said, gently chastising her pompous friend.

Lady Dunmore's face softened. "Yes, you're right, of course, Nora. You've always been so sensible."

Justine tried to involve Monique in a conversation to make her feel more at ease, but she only replied in monosyllables.

The other guests trooped in; Hoppy, full of wit and grace; Roger, glum and pale. Miss Trowbridge's voice boomed with questions about the new infant, and when the guests had been ushered into the drawing room for refreshments, Baby Diana's grandmother, the dowager countess, came downstairs carrying the infant dressed in a lace-edged white gown and a tiny muslin cap. Everyone, except the gentlemen, cooed over the girl, and the Dowager Countess Allenson took the compliments as if directed at her.

The butler announced dinner, and the guests strolled into the dining room. Damien sat next to Justine, and his presence pushed everything else from her mind. He smelled of soap and polished leather, and his grin held a hint of deep tenderness, a quirk she'd never seen before. Something had deepened between them, going beyond all the difficulties they'd faced in the past. The past did not exist, she thought. One learned, then one moved on. If their attraction held, it promised to be more than mere infatuation. The thought made her weak, and she sat down before she would slump against him.

"You look lovely," he said, that curious tenderness still lurking in his eyes. "But then you always do, lovely enough to bend the hardest heart."

"Surely, you're exaggerating, Damien," she said, finding that her voice had all but disappeared as he stared at her.

"There aren't words great enough to describe what I feel for you," he whispered, "even if I'm still disappointed that you kept the valise a secret."

Her heart jumped, then settled in a race over which she had no control. She could find nothing to say; she could only nod and stare at the other guests as they grouped themselves around the table.

Vases of yellow roses on the table sent out a sweet scent, crystal glimmered, and silver sparkled. The tablecloth of starched linen made an excellent background for the polished china. The very air seemed to glow with gaiety, and the candle flames danced in the soft draft from the open windows.

For now the air glowed. The evening would probably end on a different note, Justine thought, her magical mood slowly disappearing. Despite her love for Damien, problems remained unsolved. She could not hope for a future with him until she had all the answers to her questions.

The footmen brought around tureens with fish-and-vegetable soup. Henry made sure to keep the conversation going, and Nora looked animated and quite happy to be out of her state of seclusion.

"I daresay this is one of the happiest moments in my life," Henry said at his end of the table.

Damien lifted his glass. "A toast to the new member of the Allenson family."

"Hear, hear," everyone said, Justine joining in, even though she knew that this dinner was not only to celebrate Baby Diana's arrival but to catch a spy. Henry didn't seem perturbed, rather the opposite, as if the spy issue were something that did not greatly burden his thoughts. Mayhap the prospect of catching a spy excited him. She knew he'd spent hours with Damien trying to come up with a convincing story to present at the table.

She ate her fish-and-vegetable soup but did barely taste it. Her hand trembled, and she hoped that no one would notice her agitation.

"May you have many more children, Henry and Nora," Damien said, his voice warm. *He* didn't seem overly concerned, either.

Everyone laughed, and the footmen took away the soup plates. A dish of turbot and then salmon in almond sauce followed. Justine tasted some of each, finding the pieces of tender fish hard to swallow.

"Are you off to London soon, Lord Allenson?" Lady Dunmore asked.

"Yes, rather soon, I'm afraid," he began, "but for the time being I have light duty, only have to keep up my extensive correspondence. I have my trusty fellow Shadwell to thank for his prompt assistance." He nodded toward the secretary at the middle of the table. "He's worth his weight in gold."

Lady Dunmore muttered something under her breath. Roger sat next to her, his face morose. Justine noted that he hadn't touched his wine glass. Charity sat straight across from him, beside Hoppy. She bore a restrained expression as well, no matter how much Hoppy tried to catch her attention with whispered comments.

"I daresay I'm glad the war with France is over," said Miss Trowbridge. "The population of Oldhaven has been sadly depleted. Most able-bodied men are dead and gone. So many are struggling to survive. The women have to take care of the farms, and old men go out in the fishing boats even if they're so infirm they can barely walk." She sighed. "I do hope Wellington is making sure there won't be another war."

Henry exchanged a glance with Damien, who stiffened slightly. "Wellington is doing an outstanding job, Miss Trowbridge. His headquarters are set up at Cambrai, and the allied army is at the moment rebuilding the barrier fortresses facing Flanders. I daresay the soldiers will come back home sooner than we thought," Henry went on smoothly.

Damien found Justine's hand and squeezed it. Henry's next words would be the trap.

"I'm not at liberty to speak of my correspondence with Castlereagh in London and Wellington in Cambrai, but I daresay the Jacobins are all but rooted out in Paris thanks to the diligent Prime Minister, the Duke of Richelieu." Henry lowered his voice a notch. The perfect negotiator, Justine thought. All eyes were trained on him.

"We have discovered incendiary information that will give the death knell to the clandestine revolutionary movement. 'Twill be gone, once and for all. On both sides of the Channel. All I have to do now is send the information to certain sources, and—"

Silence invaded the room. Breaths, some rapid and

shallow, some rasping and deep, filled the eerie stillness. Justine stared at all people present, but could only detect curiosity, no furtive glances or cheeks paling with guilt.

"Are you saying there are *Englishmen* who support the dogma of Bonaparte?" the Dowager Countess Allenson asked in outraged tones.

"That is unfortunately true," Damien said. "But we have discovered certain . . . *facts*. . . ." He let the word hang as everyone looked at him gravely.

Suddenly, Henry slapped the table. "I say! This is too morbid a discussion on a lovely evening like this. I don't want to pull my friends into my tedious government business that is mostly handled by boring bulletins. My desk is full of never-ending work even as we're enjoying this meal. Enough is enough. It's an evening for entertainment."

"Has anyone read *The Present State of Roadmaking,* by John McAdam? I must say it's rather interesting," Mr. Thornton said to change the subject.

Justine did not listen to the following discussion, her thoughts swirling around the issue uppermost in her mind, the false letter in Henry's desk. Tucked into a diplomatic pouch, it would never cross the Channel or land on Wellington's desk in Cambrai. Had Henry's and Damien's "careless" revelations tickled the Fox's curiosity? She prayed that they had been suggestive enough to lure the Fox into Henry's study. The spy could be caught, and she could finally put the matter of the valise behind her.

The footmen brought in silver platters filled with roasted sirloin of beef, a haunch of venison, fowls, stuffed pigeons, and grilled poult. To end the feast after other endless rounds of side dishes, the guests tasted strawberry ices, tarts with thick creams, and currant puddings. Justine thought the meal would never end.

Finally the ladies withdrew to the drawing room for tea while the gentlemen stayed in the dining room sampling Henry's finest port. After drinking tea, Justine grew nervous.

"You look like you're sitting on an anthill, Justine," Charity said with a smile.

"I need to move around or I will resemble one of Nora's plump frien— sofas, ere long."

Charity giggled at her allusion to sofas. "Did you notice that Roger did not drink at the table?"

"Yes, mayhap he's seen the errors of his ways."

"Perhaps. Father won't let him into the house. I'm afraid that's the end of my friendship with Roger." Charity heaved a sigh.

"Do you regret it?"

Charity slowly shook her head. "No . . . he's rather sweet, but I'm not overly attracted to him."

"I hope you didn't sustain lingering pains from your adventure."

"No, I'm fit as a fiddle, as Father always says. I have the constitution of a horse. Another one of his favorite expressions."

Justine heard voices in the hallway. The gentlemen were leaving the dining room. Speaking in loud voices and laughing, they joined the ladies. Damien glanced at Justine, and her heart began that strange gallop he so easily provoked. Her heart had made that odd little dance the very first time their eyes had met.

Before long, the guests began their departure, and Justine was afraid the chance to catch the Fox had passed.

"None of the ladies left the tea table. Did you see anyone going into the study?" she whispered to Damien as he bent over her hand as if to say good-bye.

"No. Henry made sure to keep everyone together. I'll pretend to leave, then go directly to the study where Henry and I will wait in the dark until our spy arrives."

"I now doubt that he will," Justine said gloomily.

"He does not dare *not* come, my sweet. He has to find out if what Henry said is true."

Justine waved at the departing guests. The last to leave were Mr. Thornton and Charity and the group from the Crest. Roger spoke to everyone. "I'm sorry for the pain I've caused each and every one of you with my careless behavior." He bowed to Mr. Thornton. "If you can find it in your heart to forgive me, I shall not pester Miss Thornton with my presence. I have come to the conclusion that the bottle cannot save me; only I can save my life, make something of it."

His face crumpled in a most ungentlemanly manner, and Damien draped his arm protectively around Roger's shoulders and led him out to the waiting carriage.

"Poor boy, he's so unhappy," said Clara Trowbridge.

"Apparently he has learned his lesson," Henry said. He turned to Mr. Thornton. "It's kind of you not to challenge him with pistols at dawn for what he did to Charity."

Mr. Thornton grimaced. "I think he's been punished enough, and Charity is fit, aren't you, girl?"

They left, and as Nora went upstairs with Diana, Henry and Justine sneaked off to the library. "I'd rather you did not involve yourself, Justine," Henry said in the dark room. He opened the tall windows to make way for a spy bent on investigation. "But I daresay it would be futile to forbid you to stay."

"I would succumb, wither with curiosity, tear my hair out in frustration."

"Hmm, well we can't have that," Henry said, smiling grimly. "You must promise to keep quiet. No moving at all."

Damien entered promptly, and silence fell over the mansion as the last carriage pulled away from the front door.

Henry led Justine to a chair by the fireplace and pulled it behind a lacquered screen. "Sit here. Damien and I will wait close by the desk."

Justine nodded, even though he could not see her. The warm humid air brought in a scent of roses and newly scythed grass. The sky was black with clouds, not a stray star to be seen anywhere. Waiting was tedious. They might have to wait half the night before anyone dared to enter Henry's sanctuary.

Damien pushed the windows closed, leaving only a small crack. "If they are wide open, he might get suspicious."

They waited and waited. The household fell into a deeper silence as the servants climbed to the attic in search of rest. Justine could not stop herself from yawning repeatedly, and she was quite out of patience when finally one of the windows swung open on silent hinges.

The movement was almost ghostlike, and the hairs rose on her neck. Someone had entered the room so quietly she could barely discern any movement at all.

Breathless stillness, a rasp of fabric against a piece of furniture, another rasp of fabric as someone possibly raised an arm. Someone applied flint to steel in a tinderbox, and soon tinder flared, lighting the wick of a small oil lamp.

Justine peeped around the screen, her heart racing so hard she could barely breathe.

An orange flare, a glow illuminating the face of Graham Mount Hopper. Hoppy. Justine quelled an urge to step over and cuff him on the head. He'd pretended interest in her, but his goal had probably been Henry's study all along. She was glad their friendship had never taken.

Hoppy riffled through the papers on Henry's desk with a quick practiced hand. *Look in the middle drawer,* Justine urged him silently.

He finally did. He pulled out the official-looking document with several red seals dangling from the bottom. Henry had been overzealous with the wax, Justine thought, her gaze pinned on the paper. She did not dare to blink, lest she would miss one of Hoppy's moves.

He smiled, hurriedly rolling the parchment into a tube. Henry stepped quickly from behind the tall desk chair where he'd been crouching and gripped Hoppy's arm. "So you're the Fox or should I say—the second Fox?"

Damien came from the other side, but Hoppy managed to tear himself free before Damien could grip him. He vaulted over the desk and rushed to the door, which was closer than the windows.

At that moment, Shadwell opened the door carrying a branch of candles. In an instant, he seemed to understand that something was wrong and tripped Hoppy as the young man barged through.

Hoppy sprawled on the floor, and Damien and Henry got him in a firm hold. They dragged him to a chair, and

Shadwell found a piece of rope with which he bound Hoppy's hands tightly.

Hoppy swore and tried to work his hands loose. Henry pushed Hoppy's head back, pinching his jaw. "And where were you planning to sell that document, pray tell? In Paris?"

"It's none of your business," Hoppy said sullenly.

"I can tell you about your life if you don't want to confess here now," Damien said lightly. "I had a very thorough report on you from a friend at Bow Street—or should I say second report. The first one did not say much, but the second says you had an older brother in the army. You knew he supplemented his army wages with espionage for Bonaparte. He lived rather well, your brother—before he was tried by the court-marshal. He fled and sought asylum in Paris, didn't he?"

"My brother is dead!" Hoppy said.

"Yes, Daniel Mount Hopper is dead. The Fox is dead—as you well know. You didn't mind taking over where he left off, did you, Hoppy? You could pay your heavy gambling debts and finance your life of leisure in London. Costs a mint, doesn't it?" Damien paused, staring hard at the sullen spy. "What I don't understand is, how did you contact the French after Boney left for St. Helena?"

Hoppy did not answer.

"I think I can tell you that, as I have done a bit of investigation on my own," Henry said. "Through a very radical Whig member, a friend of Daniel Hopper, a friend who served in the Peninsula with your brother, then went to work at the War Office, then came to me at the Home Office." He whirled and faced Shadwell. "My own right-hand man, Garvey Shadwell."

"How could you?" Henry roared as he gripped his secretary and twisted Shadwell's arm behind his back. "You told everyone a pack of lies, always very quiet and unassuming. Always a perfect Tory sympathizer, a royalist. You thought Hoppy would take the whole blame, didn't you? You tripped him and bound him. Is that why you came here tonight, to blame him, or did you plan to take the document yourself?"

Damien fought with Shadwell and tied him up beside Hoppy. "I daresay this is a rare night's work." He toed Hoppy's leg. "Why did you snoop through my desk at the Crest? Did you think you could find something that would incriminate me?"

Hoppy sneered. "The Crest is rather comfortable. I liked the idea of spending the summer here, so close to the Channel. Roger told me you were involved with the local smugglers. As such, you might have certain foreign information to sell."

"But you found none," Damien said.

Hoppy sneered. "I found an empty valise in Miss Bryerly's room."

Henry punched Hoppy in the mouth. "That shall teach you to sneer again!" He addressed Damien. "You'll get the local men, and we'll have these two locked up and brought before the magistrate tomorrow morning. Then it's off to Newgate to await a trial. I'll wager 'twill be the biggest case of the year." He turned to Shadwell. "I can't fully express my disappointment, my disgust with you!" Cursing, he planted a facer to his secretary's jaw.

Damien went out on the terrace and whistled. Before long, fishermen entered carrying cudgels and staffs. They did not say a word as they forced the men out through the window.

"I'll go and make sure they lock them up securely in the village," Henry said, his voice suddenly weary. He spoke again, his face twisted in a grimace. "I had plans for that young man, Shadwell. I thought he was an honorable fellow. I can't bear to see how wrong I was when judging his character."

Henry left, evidently forgetting that Justine was still present and now in a compromising situation with Damien Trowbridge.

She came out from her hiding place. "I'm speechless."

"I suppose you longed to throw yourself into the fray," Damien said, his lips curling upward.

"I was shocked. I never thought—"

"You never really know the person next to you. He can be a master spy or a king or just what he says he is—a romantic fool. Like me." He pulled her cold, trembling body into his arms and held her tightly.

"You feel so good, so right in my arms. I take this opportunity to hold you in a most ungentlemanly fashion. If you scream, Henry will come and rescue you."

"I feel no need to scream," she said, her voice muffled against his neckcloth. "I want you to hold me forever."

"The nightmare is over. There won't be any more secrets between us, and we will promise to trust each other." He tilted her face up. "Do you agree?"

"Yes," she said, captured by the tenderness in his eyes.

"I won't let you slip away from me again. This time, I'll tie you to me forever. Agreed?"

She nodded. "Agreed."

His eyebrows rose. "Really? You agree to marry me? Without my going down on my knees and offering undying devotion?"

She nodded again. "Yes, because I know you can't offer me that. Only one loving day after another. Let's pray our devotion to each other will grow, just as Henry's and Nora's has."

He closed his eyes and nuzzled her nose with his. "One day at a time. I love you, Justine. More than anything in the world."

"I love you, Damien. I always have since the first time I looked into your wicked eyes."

Filled with intense emotion, he gave a trembling sigh and squeezed his eyes shut. "This means I will have to ride into Bath and officially ask your father for your hand in marriage."

"Yes, that you must, or Henry will call you out."

Damien laughed. "I can't risk that. Henry is a bruiser with pistols."

He held her face between his hands. "I shall steal an improper kiss before someone discovers us."

"No need to steal anything," Justine said and closed her eyes as his mouth came down upon hers and their tongues mingled honey-soft and yearning. At last, Justine thought. At last she was home.

If you enjoyed this book, take advantage of this special offer. Subscribe now and...

Get a Historical

No Obligation

If you enjoy reading the very best in historical romantic fiction...romances that set back the hands of time to those bygone days with strong virile heros and passionate heroines ...then you'll want to subscribe to the True Value Historical Romance Home Subscription Service. Now that you have read one of the best historical romances around today, we're sure you'll want more of the same fiery passion, intimate romance and historical settings that set these books apart from all others.

Each month the editors of True Value select the four *very best* novels from America's leading publishers of romantic fiction. We have made arrangements for you to preview them in your home *Free* for 10 days. And with the first four books you

receive, we'll send you a FREE book as our introductory gift. No Obligation!

FREE HOME DELIVERY

We will send you the four best and newest historical romances as soon as they are published to preview FREE for 10 days (in many cases you may even get them before they arrive in the book stores). If for any reason you decide not to keep them, just return them and owe nothing. But if you like them as much as we think you will, you'll pay just $4.00 each and save at *least* $.50 each off the cover price. (Your savings are *guaranteed* to be at least $2.00 each month.) There is NO postage and handling—or other hidden charges. There are no minimum number of books to buy and you may cancel at any time.

FREE

Romance
(a $4.50 value)

Send in the Coupon Below

To get your FREE historical romance and start saving, fill out the coupon below and mail it today. As soon as we receive it we'll send you your FREE Book along with your first month's selections.
